IF
YOU
COULD
SEE...

CONSTANCE COOPER

ISBN 978-1-63630-128-0 (Paperback)
ISBN 978-1-63630-129-7 (Digital)

Covenant Books, Inc.
11661 Hwy 707
Murrells Inlet, SC 29576
www.covenantbooks.com

It was a beautiful day. The sun was shining, and there was just a whisper of a breeze—enough to keep you cool, but not so much that the dust around him released its hold on the dry ground as he strolled slowly to his truck. The seeming calmness of the day was in stark contrast to the alertness of every fiber of his being. It seemed impossible that all was so quiet. His ears strained to penetrate the peaceful silence, sure that something was lurking just at the edges of his ability to discern.

There it was, just barely audible. Was it a step? Was it something falling to the ground? As his ears strained for another sign, his eyes darted back and forth as if willing the sound to repeat. His whole body froze for only an instant as he forced himself into a seemingly unaltered next step.

Stay calm. Move naturally, he told himself.

There it was again. This time, without a moment's hesitation, he spun in the direction of the sound, his hand instinctively going to his hip. Instantly, his eyes zeroed in on the source of the sound, and in the same instant, his hand and body relaxed.

"Charis! You have to quit doing that!" he only half-jokingly barked at the source of the sound.

The slightly overweight American shorthair rose from her stalking crouch at the sound of his voice. Her ears drooped at the hint of disapproval. Her bright blue eyes widened as if to peer deeply into the blue eyes looking back at her.

He almost imperceptibly shook his head as every muscle in his body relaxed. "You are a mess, little lady. Do you even realize…" He let his voice trail off, half scolding himself for talking to a cat, half trying to realize what she had just caused.

It seemed to be happening more lately. The smallest thing— sound, sight—could set him off.

He squatted to the ground and held his arms out to the gray-and-white ball of fur. Her entire demeanor turned from questioning to complete joy. Immediately, she stood and, in an almost bunny-like hop, bounded toward him. Watching her always brought a tinge of pity. This little three-legged stalker could always make his day better. As she jumped into his arms, he whispered her name.

"Charis. You know that means grace. You always remind me that's what I need. Oh, God," he spoke audibly to the sky, "I need your grace." As the words passed from audible to inaudible, he continued, "I can't keep reacting that way. I need your help to readjust. Help me find a way to cope or a person to share this with. By your grace, you took my sin. Take this too."

He looked back down at the cat in his arms. "You have to stay here. I need to go get some gas for my truck."

He set her down and walked the few steps back to his vehicle. Once behind the wheel, he looked around him at the beautiful countryside. The beauty of the day and the scenery around him now began to sink in. As the calm of his surroundings invaded his senses, it seemed to impart peace to his very being. With a large sigh of relief, he looked heavenward with a "thank you," knowing that God had heard.

Ezekiel Christian was finally home. He was home after years of service. His almost black curly hair and sun-darkened skin had made him perfect for his job. An almost perpetual five-o'clock shadow gave him the ability to grow a beard almost at a moment's notice. Add to that a six-foot frame and athletic build, he seemed destined for a career in the military. The only thing that belied his true identity as he tried to slip by unnoticed in the Middle East were those blue eyes.

That was an easy fix, however. He didn't need contacts for his 20/20, but he wore them to mask those eyes. He'd been told they were his best feature, his most expressive anyway. His grandmother had always told him to look into people's eyes when they were talking. She said they were the windows to the soul. It had been his experience that Granny was right. He wasn't sure if her ability to read his mind had come from looking in his eyes or if that was just one of those God-given gifts that all mothers had and perfected by the time they were grandmothers. Either way, it had become his practice to pay close attention to a person's eyes. Perhaps, that's why others often commented on his eyes.

Suddenly, from just past his peripheral vision on his left, a motorcycle sped alongside him. This was just a two-lane road. What was that guy doing? The cycler darted in front of his truck, waving at him with a single finger as he zoomed on his way. Looking down at his speedometer, he saw that he was actually going about five miles over the speed limit. Ezekiel shook his head. "What's happened to people today? I think everybody is so self-absorbed they don't even realize how obnoxious they are!" He continued to fume about the vulgarity of people as he turned into the lot at the gas station.

Every pump was full, and lines of cars stretched from each one. Where did all these people come from? As impatient people darted to and fro to get the next pump, he continued to fume about how people just didn't care anymore.

She'd been waiting awhile, but that wasn't a big deal. It was summer; school was out, and as a teacher, she felt free to just wait. She loved her job. She loved her students, but she was also thankful for a break. As she waited for the cars in front of her to finish filling up, she hummed along to the song on the radio.

"Eeeeek!" The squealing of tires startled her from her daydream. A couple of young men sped off in their sports car, with speakers thumping and fists pumping. In their wake, a grocery cart lay dented, and its contents scattered across the parking lot. An elderly woman stood with her hands over her mouth, reacting in shock to what had just happened.

Without hesitation, Cory quickly maneuvered out of line and over to the woman. She hopped out of her car and rushed to help.

"Are you okay?" she comforted

"I'm fine. It's a good thing I was having trouble finding my keys. I had let go of my cart. I guess it rolled into the driving lane."

"I don't think this was your fault. Those boys were being really reckless. I'm just glad you're okay. My name is Cory. Let me help you see what we can salvage"

"Oh, God is always looking out for this old lady! Thank you, Cory. My name is Naomi. I'm sure everything is fine, but I welcome the help."

The two ladies began to gather the groceries that were scattered and rolling around on the ground. They laughed and joked as they chased the especially stubborn cans.

See! thought Ezekiel as he glared at the two punks racing away in their car. "Oh, you're so tough. Mommy and Daddy are probably paying for that hunk of junk. You must feel sooooo tough running over an old lady. That's exactly the freedoms the boys and I are fighting for you to have! You wouldn't be so tough on the battlefield!"

Looking skyward, he continued his rant. "That's exactly what I mean. We're out there risking our lives, and for what? Punks like that? Aren't there any true Christians anymore? Doesn't anybody care?"

He pounded his steering wheel in disgust. As he did, his eyes lowered to level, and he peered out the windshield. There in front of him, two ladies laughed as they picked up the groceries which had been scattered by the reckless vehicle. He watched, amazed. They laughed. They weren't mad or hurt. They laughed.

"Aren't there any true Christians anymore? Doesn't anybody care?" His words echoed back at him. Shame washed over him as the hypocrisy of his statement coupled with his inactivity dawned on him. In a fluid motion, he put his truck in gear, pulled out of line, and moved over to the parking lot.

"I think some stuff rolled over here." Cory moved to the other side of the car. "Oh no," she said under her breath as her eyes fell on a punctured half gallon of milk sticking halfway out from under the front tire. Kneeling to the ground, she stretched to grab the milk. When she did, she noticed a carton of eggs. Milk in hand, she reached for the eggs.

But she wasn't the only one.

"Here, let me," Ezekiel offered.

"Oh!" Startled, she let go of the carton and drew her hand back.

"I didn't mean to startle you," he whispered. "Is she missing anything else?"

Cory looked up into possibly the bluest eyes she had ever seen. They were smiling. "I...think everything but the eggs and this milk survived," she answered, lifting the punctured carton.

"Stall her, and I'll go get replacements." He volunteered as he turned and rushed into the store.

Cory sat stunned, watching him disappear behind the automated doors. *What just happened? Wow, he was good looking! Who was that?* Thoughts swirled in her head. *Things like this don't happen to me.*

"Cory? Where are you, dear?" Naomi's voice broke into her stupor.

"I'm here," she answered. *I've got to stall,* she thought. "I think some cans rolled under these cars over here." She stood, caught Naomi's gaze, and pointed to some cars nearby.

"I guess that could have happened. I really don't remember everything I purchased. Let's look," the elderly woman stated as she smiled at Cory.

"You know, Ms. Naomi, you have a great smile. I think I'm glad those boys about ran you over!" Cory said jokingly.

"Well, I think God sent the excitement so I could meet you and be reminded what it feels like to get my heart pumping!" She giggled. The two started searching around the cars.

Cory spotted a rogue can of green beans and kicked it under a small Toyota. "Look! I found a can. I'll just get down here and see if I can reach it." She knew she could but took her time getting to it. As she looked under the car, she saw some boots, then a knee, and then...there were those eyes again.

"Good job. I'm back," he whispered under the car. Then he stood and said, "Excuse me, do these belong to you?"

"Oh! I forgot all about my milk and eggs. How in the world did they get over there?" She queried as she looked over at Cory rising from the ground with the green beans in her hand.

"Here you go," Ezekiel handed her the eggs. She opened them and checked each one.

"Hmmm. I wonder how they got over here without breaking," she asked with a highly skeptical tone. "The milk too. I think perhaps God has been watching over me." There was a twinkle in her eye.

Ezekiel and Cory looked at one another. "Busted." They smiled together.

"Well, all I can say is that today, God reminded me that He is still watching, and He sent you two angels to make an old woman's day." She grabbed each one by the hand and brought their hands together. "I guess you could say I'm glad those naughty boys sped past me today! You two have restored my hope in young people. Now, pass it on to hoodlums like those two." Hugging each one, she loaded the last of her groceries into her car and drove away smiling and waving.

Cory and Ezekiel stared after her as she drove away. Awkwardly, they looked back at each other.

"Thank you," Cory offered.

"No, thank you. I'm only sorry I didn't react as quickly as you did to help." Ezekiel confessed.

"But you did react. That's what matters. Besides that, I only crawled around under cars. You put your money where your mouth was!" Cory chuckled nervously.

Ezekiel just smiled as their eyes met.

"Well, at least, I won't have to wait in line for gas now." Cory motioned to the pumps. "I better get going. Thanks again."

Ezekiel nodded, and the two parted ways.

Cory pulled her truck up to the pump, turned off the key, and got her Kroger Cares card. Most people would pay with a debit card, but not Cory. She didn't use cards. She had gotten into money trouble using cards, so it was strictly cash or check now. She pulled a twenty out of her wallet and made her way to the window.

"Twenty on pump 4," she said as she smiled at the clerk.

The clerk pushed the money back at her. "It's already been taken care of. You can begin pumping." He smiled.

"What?" Cory said confused,

"Ask him," the clerk explained. "He said he was rewarding a Good Samaritan."

Looking to the pump, there stood the man, smiling. Determinedly, Cory marched back to her truck. "Look, I appreciate the gesture, but you don't have to do this," she scolded.

Surprised, he responded, "It's okay. I just want to thank you."

"I appreciate that, but I really can't accept. I didn't help Naomi so that I could get something."

"I know that. It's just that I had spent the whole day griping about how nobody cared anymore, and you proved me wrong."

"I'm glad I could help, but I really can't let you spend money on me," she said firmly.

Ezekiel and Cory faced off, determined.

Cory peered into those blue eyes. She recognized stubbornness when she saw it. Her father, an old marine, would get that look in his eyes. When he did, there was no changing his mind. She knew she wasn't going to win this standoff, but she was going to get something.

"Okay, I can see I'm not going to win this argument, but I'll only let you pay for my gas if you answer a question to my satisfaction." She looked defiantly up at him and squared her shoulders to communicate her determination.

Ezekiel smiled down at her. *She's got some spunk. I never dreamed she wouldn't let me buy her some fuel. I'm intrigued.* "Okay. Ask away."

"If you were to die tonight, do you know where you would go?"

Pleasantly surprised, he gladly responded, "I would go to heaven."

"How do you know?"

"Wait a minute," Ezekiel smiled. "I thought you said one question?"

"I said to my satisfaction, and I'm not satisfied yet."

Ezekiel's smile widened. *I just want to buy her some fuel, and she wants to know about my eternity. I think I like this girl,* he thought.

"Okay," he verbalized. "I know that I will spend my eternity in heaven because when I was ten, I realized that I didn't deserve to be loved by God, much less to go to heaven. My parents were missionaries to the Aborigines in Australia, so I had heard often about God's plan for salvation. I was on a hunt in the bush, and I made my first kill. As I looked at that dead animal, I began to realize that, one day, I would die too. I knew I needed Jesus, so right there, I asked Him to forgive me of my sins and come into my heart. He did. I know His promises are true, so I know I will spend eternity in heaven."

Cory's smile spread across her face but glowed from her heart. "I guess that answers my question."

"If you are satisfied, does that mean I get to buy you fuel?"

"We had a deal," she said as she moved to take off the gas cap. "How'd you get here from Australia?"

"Well, it's a long story, but to make it short, I've just taken a professorship at the seminary. I'll be teaching courses for chaplains. I'm a chaplain for the special forces."

"Southwestern? Really? Wow. I guess I never thought about how they trained chaplains, but I have heard that they've kinda been under attack lately."

"You're right. It can be hard with all the stateside bickering, but out in the field, chaplains are indispensable. I know. I'm still on active duty. This is just a sabbatical."

"Well, I get the feeling there's a much deeper story there, but I won't pry. Thanks for your service."

Thunk.

"Looks like it's full," Ezekiel said as he topped off the tank. "Listen, I don't want to sound like a stalker or anything, but they're having a get-together for the professors on Friday, and I don't know anyone here. Would you consider helping me out by going with me?"

"Help you out?" Cory asked

"This may sound pathetic, but ever since I got here, all the wives have been trying to set me up, and all the single female professors…well, you know. I've really enjoyed your company and just thought…" His voice trailed off. *I must sound like a creep*, he thought.

"I can sympathize. I've been in the ministry for a long time, and people at church seem to feel it is their mission to give me relationship advice."

"It's at the seminary, and it's informal. I could even provide the T-shirt. It's a matching shirt party."

"Okay, just two conditions," she replied.

"Sure, anything," he said hopefully.

"Well, I'll meet you at the seminary, and I'll need to know your name." She smiled.

"Oh, I'm Ezekiel. Ezekiel Christian," he said, offering his hand.

"Okay, Mr. Christian. I'm Cory. Cory Carter. What time do I need to be there?" she said, thinking, *I can't believe I'm doing this!*

"Six thirty. That should be perfect, and you can leave if you feel uncomfortable. I...well, this is new to me. Thanks."

The two shook hands and said their goodbyes.

I can't believe I'm doing this, Cory scolded herself as she drove toward the seminary. *This NEVER happens to me! Please, God, don't let this be a bad idea. I mean, I'm headed to the seminary. How bad could it be?*

The fear and doubts continued to swirl as she drove. She was right. She had no experience with men. In fact, she always felt uncomfortable around people her own age. She was fine around teenagers. She had spent the last twenty years of her life as a youth minister in small Baptist churches. All through college, her weekends weren't spent out with friends; they were spent on retreats or teaching Sunday school to seventh through twelfth graders. When she finally got a job, it was as a teacher and coach in a middle school. During the summers, she worked at summer camps for youth, teaching Bible study and playing lots of volleyball.

It had never been her plan to work in the church. In high school, she had dreamed of getting married and having children of her own. It just hadn't worked out that way. She had attended three high schools as her family moved around, and the church she attended in college didn't have anyone to teach in the youth department, so she did it. That began a long string of finding herself in situations where there was no one else to help out at church. She just couldn't look the other way. They needed her, and well, it felt good to be needed.

As her thoughts swirled, she pulled into the familiar parking lot and whispered a prayer.

"Oh, God, protect me."

Before she could finish, she heard a knock on the window. Putting the car in park, she looked up from the wheel. His eyes twinkled, and the smile on his face was contagious, and one spread across her own.

Here goes nothing, she thought as she opened the door.

"I'm so glad you made it." He smiled. "I was so afraid maybe I scared you off."

"Well, I have to admit, I have never been accused of being spontaneous. This has to top the list."

"Truth be told, I'm pretty much a fuddy duddy, but I just don't think I could make it through another one of these get-togethers with everyone trying to set me up. It's been a long time since I enjoyed talking with someone like I did with you yesterday. The idea just kinda hit me, so I guess we'll be trying out spontaneity together," he confessed.

"Sounds good." Cory looked down at his shirt. It was her favorite shade of purple with the word "STUPID" boldly printed across the front. "You said something about a matching-shirt party?"

"Yeah, I'm not too original, but here's your T-shirt." He held out one in a matching shade of purple. Emblazoned on it were the words "I'M WITH STUPID."

Cory just giggled. "I haven't seen one of those in a long time."

"I know it's lame, but if I were to come up with something original, I might hurt myself. Some of these old professors might drop over dead if I showed up with a date AND a creative idea!" He responded with a chuckle of his own.

"I'll just slip it on over my shirt," she narrated as she reached for the shirt.

"Here," he offered, "let me help."

As he held the shirt to help her put it on, a voice came from behind him.

"There you are."

It was a feminine voice. As Cory's head emerged through the neck hole, she saw the look on Ezekiel's face. He looked as if he had just swallowed something sour.

"Oh, no," he breathed out, then looked pleadingly at Cory. "Please play along."

The look in his eyes convinced her of his desperation, so she merely nodded.

"I was waiting for you inside. I have absolutely no idea why you are still out here," the voice continued.

Cory realized that she couldn't be seen from the other side of Ezekiel. His body was completely blocking her from the view of this person.

"Amber," he turned and spoke. "I don't know why you were waiting for me. I told you I was bringing someone."

"I know, but you always say that. Then you have some excuse why you arrive alone. You don't have to worry about being alone. I'm always here for you," the voice added.

Just as Amber reached for him, Ezekiel stepped aside, revealing Cory.

"Amber, this is Cory"—he shot Cory that pleading glance—"my girlfriend."

The word caught her off guard, but only for a moment. With seemingly no hesitation, she shot her hand out to the woman and smiled. "So you must be the one he was telling me about. It's nice to meet you."

Amber stared at Cory, stunned, but reached out for the out-stretched hand as if by instinct alone. It was evident that she was completely unprepared for the sight of a woman with Ezekiel. Her eyes took in the matching shirts as if to confirm that they were together.

"Well," she finally broke the silence, "I guess Ezekiel was telling the truth. How long have you known him?"

"Oh, we've known each other for a while…" Cory began, not exactly telling a lie.

"Yeah, I'd say God brought us together at just the right time, and we have been taking it one step at a time since then." Ezekiel finished for her. He too was straining to avoid a complete lie.

"I suppose we should really head inside," Cory deflected. "I apologize that I kept him out here so long that you came looking for him. That was terribly rude of me."

"It's okay," Ezekiel added as he took her by the hand. "You're here now, and that's what matters. Let's go inside."

He shot Cory a covert glance that conveyed both apology and thanks. She reciprocated and offered a smile.

The trio walked without another word into the lobby of the building. There, they were met with festively decorated tables and small groupings of people amiably chatting with one another. One elderly couple detached from their group and moved toward them with purpose, smiling as they came. The man was wearing a T-shirt with what looked like garbage or trash pictured on the front. The woman's shirt was obscured by the vest she wore.

"Mr. Christian!" the woman proclaimed as she reached out to hug him. "I was beginning to fear that you weren't coming. So we finally get to meet her." She embraced Cory with a smile and a wink.

"You know about her?" Amber asked, obviously skeptical.

"Why, of course, I do. Ezekiel hasn't stopped talking about Cory since they met. You should know he can't keep a secret from this old lady. Now, off with you, Amber. They were looking for you to finalize the plans for the photograph."

With that, Amber had been dismissed by this precious old lady, and she moved off toward the stage. The lady then turned to Cory with a knowing look.

"Don't you worry about her, dear. She's been like a shark circling Ezekiel ever since God sent him our way." Looking to Ezekiel, she continued, "He's been ably staying just a step ahead of her. Now you boys need to go get ready for the program. Cory and I have some talking to do."

The men walked away, and the woman took Cory by the arm and directed her to a more isolated spot. Cory was a bit overwhelmed. What exactly was happening?

Her question must have been written on her face because the woman immediately began comforting. "Sorry about all that. I'm Mrs. Geoffrey. You can call me Grace. Ezekiel really has told me about you. I've made it my mission to take care of that clueless boy, well, clueless about women anyway. My husband has been teaching here at the seminary for a long time, and I've seen a lot of young men come and go. None has impressed me like this young man—I guess he's not really that young, but to me, most everybody is young."

Her kind smile and continued dialogue seemed to ease Cory.

"He is so focused on what God is doing and has a real hunger for God. I love to listen to him sit and talk with my husband. He's not just humoring the head of the department. He really has a hunger for God. When we were talking about this get-together, he told me about your meeting. I couldn't believe he had the sense to invite you to come. You stick close to me, and I'll take care of you."

Cory had the overwhelming feeling that she would do just that. She whispered a "thank you" to God.

Just then, there was a commotion near where a piano had been set up. It was Mr. Geoffrey. He was obviously frustrated and was gesturing as if trying to explain something.

"Oh, heavens, we better go see what's up."

"You know the one I'm talking about. It's an old hymn. I think it's Scottish or something. Ohhh…" Mr. Geoffrey let his words trail off in disgust. Then, seeing Grace, asked, "Dear, what is the name of that song I like so much. I want Ezekiel to play it, but I can't think of it, and no one seems to know what I'm talking about."

Looks like she has the spiritual gift of coming to everybody's rescue, thought Cory.

"Honey, calm down a minute and think. There are lots of hymns that you love. Do you remember any of the words or maybe the tune?" she cajoled.

"Oh, people today just don't sing hymns anymore. If they did, they would know. I really want to sing it tonight, but I can't seem to remember. It was something about vision, I think," he huffed as his wife took him by the hand.

Immediately, Cory knew what hymn he was talking about, but the title seemed just at the tip of her tongue. She loved hymns— that's what she grew up singing, and they still sang them at her small church. *Oh, what was the name of that song? It wasn't Scottish. It had a Celtic feel to it.* Softly, she began to hum it.

"That's it!" Mr. Geoffrey shouted as he moved closer to Cory. "That's the song. Do you know it?"

"I'm trying to remember." Then it came to her, and she burst into song. "Be Thou my vision, oh Lord of my heart..."

The room quieted as the haunting tones poured beautifully from her lips. Her eyes rose to meet those beautiful blue eyes she had begun to recognize and enjoy. As they did, he began playing along. She walked over to the piano where he sat, continuing the hymn and beginning to be lost in worship as she sang those words. The room hushed as the people moved near to hear. Mr. and Mrs. Geoffrey stood closely to one another and leaned over the piano, beaming.

As the song came to an end, Cory felt a flush come over her face. That always happened when she worshipped as she sang. It wasn't embarrassment; it was a kind of afterglow from her time with God. She had always liked that feeling. As she basked in it, Mr. Geoffrey broke in.

"How marvelous! You have the voice of an angel, and you know my song!" The chubby little man seemed utterly ecstatic. "Ezekiel, the two of you should sing something together."

"I'm game if you are, Cory. What's another song you know?" Ezekiel asked.

"There are too many to count. What about you, Mr. Geoffrey? Mrs. Geo... Grace?" Cory responded.

"I always loved 'Victory in Jesus'. Do you know that one?" Grace asked hopefully.

Ezekiel immediately began to play. Taking her cue from him, Cory jumped right in after the introduction. Ezekiel joined her in harmony on the chorus. The two sounded as if they had been singing together for ages. In a room full of professors, not one could resist the draw of the presence of the Spirit in the song.

Recognizing the power of God's presence, Cory broke from the song to invite those now gathered around the piano to join on the chorus. The room soon filled with the sound of God's people worshipping in song. They moved from one song to the next as person after person suggested favorite hymns to sing. Cory and Ezekiel knew every single one and led the impromptu worship service. Soon, even the staff preparing the food had joined the group, and there was no distinction between server and servee as they found equal place at the foot of the cross in worship. The plans for a program went out the window as God imposed His own plan for the evening.

As the "service" wound down, Mr. Geoffrey shared an impromptu word from God and then looked directly at Cory.

"Let's end tonight with a song of your choice. What would God have you share with us?"

An instant of shock and fear hit Cory. She looked out at the faces around her, aglow with the same flush she always experienced from God's presence, and those negative emotions, so out of place here, ebbed away. Without hesitation she knew what she was to sing.

"I had the incredible honor of being raised by godly parents, and though my precious mother was plagued with health problems and is gone from us today, she always had a song on her heart and one in particular became her anthem. Z, I'm sure you know this, but she did a little something at the end, so watch me."

He nodded and smiled.

"Shackled by a heavy burden..." She began the song "He Touched Me," the inspirational hymn penned by Bill and Gloria Gaither. Ezekiel found the key and seamlessly joined her song. Nodding to him after the first chorus, Ezekiel took the lead and sang the second verse, with Cory switching to harmony. As they reached the end of the second chorus, she walked to his side, touched him on the shoulder and, before the song could end, added—as her mother had—"His name is wonderful / His name is wonderful..." With fluidity, the piano rolled into the familiar chorus. Cory nodded encouragingly to those gathered, and they joined in.

"He's the Great Shepherd, the Rock of all Ages..." The room resounded with the praise.

As this song ended, Cory sat next to Ezekiel on the bench.

"His name is wonderful, Jesus my Lord / And He touched me, Oh, He touched me..." The song wound back into the chorus of the first song, and the voices followed her lead. As they finally reached their song's end, it seemed as if heaven had opened up, and all of Glory was leaning in to hear. Everyone burst into claps of praise as the last strains of music faded into the night. No one wanted to move. No one wanted to stop the feeling they had inside. For a moment, there seemed nothing but God and all His glory.

Ezekiel stood. His deep, rich, baritone voice reverently addressed the God they all had been worshipping. Every head in the room bowed in response, and a unified cry went up to heaven on behalf of these men and women who found themselves chosen to share Christ in so many different ways at the seminary. A chorus, no less grand than the singing, began as person after person spoke with God. The prayers were varied—prayers for the professors and guidance, prayers for students and encouragement, prayers for the country and revival.

When the last voice finally became silent, Mr. Geoffrey rose from the kneeling position he had taken.

"Well, my friends, that's what happens when God takes over! I suppose we should move to our tables and have something to eat, even though I think we all understand a little better what Jesus meant when He told his disciples that He had bread they knew not of."

Slowly, one-by-one, they moved to tables. Ezekiel stood and took Cory by the hand.

"Let's make sure we get a table with the Geoffrey's," he whispered and guided her to where Grace had pulled out a chair.

As if reading his mind, she said, "Don't you worry. I was getting ready to save you two a seat, and there are only four chairs at this table!" She chuckled as she saw the relief on Ezekiel's face. "Come, dear"—she took Cory's other hand—"let's run to the ladies' room to wash up."

Following her lead, Cory let her hand slip from Ezekiel's and moved to the back of the room. As the two women neared the restroom, voices could be heard from inside.

"Did you hear her? What disrespect is that? Not only does she just take over like she runs the show, she called Mr. Christian 'Z'. Who does she think she is?" Amber pushed out the door right into Cory and Grace.

Stunned, she tried to maintain her dignity. "Oh, I didn't know you were here. I guess I should ask you. Where in the world did you get the idea to call Ezekiel 'Z'?"

A voice came from behind Cory. "That's her nickname for me, and I like it. I don't see that it's any business of yours what she calls me. Besides, she's important enough to me to have earned the right to call me what she likes."

Cory turned to see "Z" standing behind her. Amber, aptly scolded, slunk quietly away. When she was gone, Cory apologized.

"I'm sorry. I didn't mean any disrespect. It just came out. It seemed like it fit. You don't have to pretend to like it. I won't use it again."

"No!" he protested. "I like it. I've always wanted a nickname but hated it when people called me Zeke." He made a face. "I really like Z. It sounds cool." Leaning closer, he whispered in her ear, "And I meant what I said about you earning the right to call me what you want."

With that, he walked past her and into the men's room to wash up before eating.

Cory stared at the door for a moment. She needed to let all that was happening sink in.

"Dear, I think it would look better if you went in the women's room and stared at the mirror instead of at the men's room door." Grace jokingly jabbed.

The two women laughed and entered the women's room.

"I kinda like 'Z' myself," Grace offered. "You know, I've never seen him this way before. I'm really glad you decided to come tonight. I hope you realize that after that little impromptu worship service, there can be no doubt that God brought you here. I think I'm excited to see what God has in store next!"

Cory smiled at the sweet woman, "Me, too, Grace. Me, too."

The duo entered the bathroom, and as Grace began to wash her hands, her vest parted, and Cory could see her T-shirt. Grace saw her looking and opened the vest so she could see the shirt.

"What do you think?" Grace asked. "Do you get it?"

Cory remembered the shirt with the trash on the front that Mr. Geoffrey was wearing. Grace had a grocery bag on her shirt.

"Let's see…" She thought aloud. "Trash and grocery bag. Oh, I get it. Trash bag!"

"You are the first one tonight to get it." Grace burst out laughing. "I guess it was a lot funnier to me and the old man."

The two women finished washing up and exited laughing.

Heading back to the table, the women joined the men who were already seated. A wonderful meal was served, and the quartet chatted the night away. From the outside it seemed the four had known each other forever. Their discussions moved fluidly from personal stories to theological discussions to politics. Each subject liberally dosed with quick wit and insight and accompanied by the delightful strains of genuine laughter. By evening's end Ezekiel and Cory had probably learned more about each other than they could have on a month's worth of "real" dates.

Just before everyone was ready to leave, Amber stood and got everyone's attention.

"Before you go, it's time for the alumni photograph for tonight's event." She began organizing all of the people for the picture.

Cory's table rose and headed for the group.

"Come on," Ezekiel called to Cory.

Amber reacted immediately, putting her hand up like a stop sign. "I'm sorry, you'll have to stand over there while Ezekiel stands next to me. The photograph is only for alumni," she said with an air of superiority.

Grace was behind Cory and whispered where only she could hear. "Don't let her talk to you like that."

Cory's back stiffened. "I am an alumnus," she stated proudly.

Amber froze and shot her a skeptical glance. "You are?"

"That's right," Mr. Geoffrey chimed in as he took his place in the picture. "Class of 1997. Now, Cory, get up here next to Ezekiel and let's get this picture taken."

As Amber turned, properly chastened, Cory took Ezekiel's hand and stood next to him on the second row.

"Well played," Ezekiel whispered through his smile.

The photographer went through a series of cameras and poses. When he was finally satisfied, he offered his thanks, and the people scattered, gathering in small groups, pleasantly chatting. Slowly, they would say their goodbyes and leave for the evening.

As the room around them emptied, the Geoffrey's came over and said their goodnights and left Ezekiel and Cory walking out to the parking lot.

"What a night," Ezekiel offered. "I'm really glad I didn't freak you out at the gas station. I can't imagine what tonight would have been like without you. I can't say enough to express my thanks."

"You don't have to say anything. I really enjoyed tonight. I wouldn't have missed it for the world," Cory replied.

"I really don't want you to go home yet. Could we walk around campus and talk some more?" Ezekiel sheepishly asked.

Cory smiled. "I'm glad you said that because I wasn't ready for it to end either." Following his lead, she swung into step beside him.

"So can I ask you a question this time?" Ezekiel broke the silence of their stroll under the glow of streetlights and along the tree-lined sidewalk around the campus.

"Sure. What would you like to know?" Cory responded.

"Why aren't you married? I mean, I don't mean to pry, but I think you are fantastic, and I can't imagine how some guy hasn't snatched you up by now."

That wasn't the question I expected, thought Cory. "Well, I don't know really," she verbalized. "I guess it's because no one ever asked." She paused, thinking for the first time about the question.

Ezekiel continued to walk along in silence as if sensing her need for thought.

"I've never been the kind of girl who attracts a lot of male attention. I don't go on a lot of dates," she finally offered.

"Oh, come on, how many dates have you been on?"

Cory stopped walking. "Do you really want to know?"

Ezekiel squared around in front of her. "Of course, I do."

Cory paused, thinking.

"That many?" Ezekiel teased.

"No, it's just that I'm not too good at knowing what a real date is. I thought I was on a date with a guy I had worked with over the summer. We got home from camp, and he called and asked me out to dinner. I was so excited. We got to the restaurant, and he explained that the reason he asked me to dinner was because an old girlfriend had called and said that she still had feelings for him, and if he no longer cared, she was going to marry some other guy who had proposed. He just wanted my advice. It wasn't a date."

Then almost as an afterthought, she said, "Does tonight count?"

"I know this night started as you doing me a favor, but I think it turned into more. So, yeah, I'd definitely call tonight a date."

Taking a deep breath and squaring her chin as she looked up at him, she said, "One."

"One?" he repeated.

The breath drained out of her, and her chin dropped.

"I told you. I'm just not the kind of girl guys like. My mom and sister used to say that I scared them away because I was already so in love with Jesus. I figure if their fear of me is stronger than their attraction to me, then I'm better off that they never asked. It's kinda hard to get a guy to ask you to marry him if he won't even ask you on a date." The words seemed to roll out as she thought how pathetic she sounded.

The raw honesty in her words drew him to her. He positioned himself so she would look at him as he spoke. "Let me say this—and I'm a guy, so I should know—you are the kind of girl guys like. The truth is, if guys were scared because of your love for Jesus, they didn't deserve you. I'm not the only one in that room who could see that you have an amazing heart for God. Every person in there loves God, and when they saw Him in you, they were drawn to you. No guy who fears your love of Jesus could ever love you like you deserve to be loved. God wouldn't do that to you." His words trailed off as he peered into her eyes. The honesty and innocence he saw there touched him. Deeply. He had seen such harshness on the battlefield. Man's depravity. Yet looking into her eyes, all that faded away. It did still exist—that precious innocence of soul awash in the grace of

God. He couldn't stop the smile that was spreading across his face, nor was he aware of the fire that flickered to life in his own eyes.

He wasn't aware, but Cory saw it. When he began to speak, she was embarrassed to look in his eyes, but as he spoke, he seemed to say what she needed to hear. It was what God had said to her many times before and she reminded herself of often, but she couldn't seem to keep the thoughts of inadequacy away—until now. What she saw in his eyes was more than the kind words of someone who felt sorry for her. God had sent those words—through Z.

"What about you?" Cory's question broke into the moment. "Why aren't you married? Why hasn't some beautiful woman wrapped you around her finger by now?"

Ezekiel smiled and turned to begin to walk. Cory immediately fell in stride beside him.

"Well," he said after a moment, "I've never met anyone I wanted to marry. Oh, I've dated, but not in a long time. When I came back to America for college, I jumped into the whole college scene. I had a different date every night." He stopped walking and looked at Cory "Oh, that sounded bad."

"No, I get it, go on." she inserted, and they walked once more.

"Well, I felt like all these girls were pushing me to do things I didn't want to do. They were trying to push me into a relationship I didn't want, to manipulate me. The guys around me let them do it. They let them objectify themselves. I couldn't. I mean, in the tribes, couples found each other because they fit. They worked together to survive. They drew strength from each other. I felt like the people around me were using each other's weaknesses to get what they wanted. I don't mean to be vulgar, but I grew up with women who didn't wear shirts, so some girl flashing her cleavage at me wasn't a turn on." Suddenly, he felt the awkwardness of the subject. He stopped walking again.

"I mean, I love a girl with nice..." His voice trailed off as his eyes involuntarily moved to her shirt.

"I mean..."

She hadn't missed the movement of his eyes. In a way, it was flattering. She jumped to his rescue, trying to pretend she was oblivious.

"I get it. Girls can be terribly manipulative. Especially when there is a man involved."

"Yeah," he quickly regained his composure, surprised. He hadn't noticed a woman like that in a long time. "Well, I found myself frustrated with a lot of things. In the outback, I had felt God call me—not to be a preacher like my Dad, but I had no doubt he wanted to use me. That coupled with my dating frustrations caused me to look for other opportunities. I found the military. Growing up as I did, I learned early the skills to survive and fight. The military was the perfect fit. I excelled and was quickly steered toward the Special Forces. There I saw my brothers struggle in relationships. I watched wives and girlfriends beg them to leave the service. I saw families sick with worry and fear; children growing up with the constant threat of losing a father—or without one at all. I just knew I couldn't put someone I love through those things, so I made a deal with God. I asked Him to hold my heart. I knew He wanted me in the services, so I told Him I would serve if He would hold my heart. And He has. I honestly haven't noticed women…until I met you. I think this is the first date I have been on in years. I know it is."

Ezekiel couldn't believe he had said all that. He never spoke this much. He didn't even realize what he felt until the words came out. What was happening?

Cory walked on in silence. Was this really happening? She had never been so honest or had someone be so honest to her before. It was frightening and a bit awkward, but it was right.

A comfortable quiet passed between them as they walked back toward the parking lot. Neither felt the need to fill the space with empty chatter. They just soaked in the moment—the night, the company, the rightness.

"Well, I'm really glad we decided to do something spontaneous tonight." Cory offered when they reached her car. To herself she thought, *We may have been spontaneous, but I have the sense that not one thing about tonight was spontaneous to God!*

"Me, too. Thanks again for coming to my rescue." He smiled as he opened her door.

"It was my pleasure," she chimed in, climbing behind the wheel.

Before he moved to shut the door, he blurted, "I really want to see you again. Could I have your number?"

Cory laughed. "Sure, but I don't own a cell, so you'll get an answering machine for the school when you call. Don't let that discourage you. Just leave a message, and I'll pick it up if I'm there or call you back when I can." Realizing how that may have sounded, she quickly added, "I'm not blowing you off. I want to see you again. I just have a thing about phones. That's a topic for our next..." She searched for the word.

"Date." He filled in the blank for her. "You can say it. That's what I'd call it. And don't worry. I've faced down terrorists. An answering machine won't scare me away. Besides, now I'm intrigued. You can bet I will be getting in touch."

Cory gave him a business card from the school. Their eyes met.

"Good night."

"Good night."

It had been a few days since the night at the seminary. Cory just couldn't seem to wipe the smile off of her face. She really had never experienced anything like what happened that weekend. She hadn't slept at all the night of the party. She spent the night writing in her journal and thanking God.

Every night since she was a child, she had written in her journal. It wasn't a diary. It was just a way of writing down her prayers to God. She had suffered with horrible nightmares as a child. Her mother had encouraged her to read her Bible and pray before she went to bed. After a while, she went to her mother and admitted that she was trying to read her Bible every night, but she kept falling asleep. Instead of scolding her, her mother had asked her if the nightmares had gone away. They had. Her mother encouraged her to keep going "because," she said, "what better way to go to sleep than with the word of God filling your mind!" From that moment on, Cory had spent time with God before going to bed each night. As she reached her teen years, her mother had purchased a journal for her. Her quiet time had gained a new dimension as she wrote out her prayers to God.

That was a long time ago. God had walked with her through many ups and downs. The pages of the journals in her closet were full of every emotion imaginable—joy, thankfulness, questions, doubts, and even tears. Through it all, God had never left her side. She knew beyond the shadow of a doubt that He would never leave her or forsake her. Maybe everything hadn't turned out as she had expected, but nothing she had gone through had knocked God off of His throne, and nothing would!

In the midst of her pleasant musing, the phone rang. Her heart froze as it always did when the phone rang. She walked over but didn't recognize the number, so she waited for the answering machine to finish.

"Hello, Cory? This is Ezekiel," the voice explained.

Stunned, she almost didn't pick it up.

"Hello, I'm here," she stammered over his message. "Hello, do you hear me? Don't hang up."

He blurted apologetically, "I hear you. Listen, I don't have much time, and I apologize for the abruptness of this call. I wanted to call and set up another date, but I've just been called out on active duty. I'm really sorry. I have to go and don't know when I'll be back. All I can say is it's important—"

"It's okay," she interrupted him. "You don't have to explain anything to me, and you definitely don't have to apologize. You told me you believed this is what God wants you to do, so that's good enough for me."

"It is?" he said, almost stunned.

"Of course. Don't you worry a bit about me. You just go, do what God wants you to do, and do it the very best you can. I'll be praying for you, and I know God will take care of us both! If you can, let the other guys know that I will be praying for all of you."

"Okay." He was speechless. He had expected questions and fear and…not this. She was actually encouraging. "I'll tell 'em, and I'll call you when I get back. Gotta go."

His face must have told the others all they needed to know. One of the guys elbowed him and smiled. "It's never easy spilling it to a new girlfriend. Just remember, you're not the only one who's lost a girl over this job."

"If she freaked, she didn't deserve ya," said another

"I'm the one who's freaked 'cuz Christian's got himself a girl to call," joked a large man with a big smile.

Finally, after loading the plane, one of his buddies sat down next to him. "Okay, who is this girl, and what did she have to say?"

"I knew there was a girl when I saw you humming while you worked out the other day. I can't believe it. Someone finally conquered the Preach," offered a camo-clad soldier.

Smiling, he explained, "Well, she's definitely not like any girl I've ever met. She told me to go do what God created me to do and to tell you guys that she's praying for us."

"What!" they articulated in almost unison.

"Yeah, she told me I didn't have to explain and not to worry. She said I didn't need to apologize," he finished, shaking his head and smiling.

"You're kidding me. You'd better marry this girl!" his commander chimed in.

"Now, wait a minute, Sarge. Is she pretty?" queried a young guy from behind him.

"Shut up, Jimmie. When you've been around as long as I have, you'll figure out that there are things more important than how pretty a girl is." Sarge scolded as he winked at Ezekiel. "Christian knows what I mean. Finding a woman who gets it, that's heaven sent."

The engines of the plane fired up. Sarge barked a few commands, and the boys were in the air, headed very few knew where. All of them carried on almost nonchalantly, but they knew their mission, and they knew they were the ones for the job. Each settled in to prepare mentally for what lay ahead.

Ezekiel said a prayer for each of them. He always did—they were headed for a life-and-death situation. This time, he couldn't help but feel more of God's presence as he prayed. In his heart, he remembered the Bible verse that talked about when two or more agreed in prayer. One verse said God was present, and another said it was settled in heaven as on earth. He couldn't help but feel God and confidence as he thought of Cory praying with him right now. He thanked God and asked for guidance and protection.

Meanwhile, Cory hung up the phone and immediately began to pray. Her heart was heavy. She wasn't afraid of what Ezekiel would face. She didn't want him to worry about her and lose focus.

"Oh, God, I know you already know what those boys are gonna face. Go before them. Use them to bring life and freedom where possible. If necessary, use them to stop evil. Guard their hearts and minds as they face whatever they must. Give Z your presence so that he can be your hands and feet to all those under his care. If they encounter nonbelievers, let your light shine through them in such a way as to open hearts to find your truth…"

She continued praying long into the night. There would be some more interesting pages in that journal of hers in the days to come as she prayed faithfully.

It had been two weeks since that phone call. Cory went outside each night as the sun was setting and spent time praying. Tonight started out no different. Her driveway led to the back of her house and sat adjacent to her backyard. They had paved a large swath of it to accommodate her mother when she became wheelchair bound. Now, there was a table and some benches sitting on the patio next to the driveway. She could sit here and watch the sun set behind the trees and houses down the street. On nights that weren't too hot, it was quite a nice spot to enjoy God's handiwork.

As she sat, just beginning her prayer time, a motorcycle pulled in her driveway and parked. She watched, wondering for a moment who it could be.

Ezekiel parked his bike, dismounted, and took off his helmet.

Cory suppressed the urge to run and throw her arms around his neck as he strode toward her. The expression on his face was enough to let her know that was inappropriate. She did, however, stand as he walked to where she was.

"Welcome home," she offered with a smile of concern, trying to catch his eyes. If she could get a look in his eyes, maybe she could see if something was wrong.

"Thanks," he answered back flatly. "Have you got a minute to talk?"

She now fully met and held his gaze. The look she found there told her he really needed to talk. She whispered a quick prayer to God and motioned for him to sit with her at the table.

Ezekiel sat astride one of the benches facing Cory. She shadowed his movement and sat astride the same bench facing him.

"I really don't know…" he began, then stopped. "I mean, I was gonna call, but I wanted to talk with you face-to-face."

He paused, but Cory felt no need to fill the space. She waited and listened.

"I really like you, but you deserve to know who I am. After you said you'd pray for me—I know you did, by the way. I felt it. But after you said I was doing what God made me to do, I got to thinking. Is this what God made me to do? I mean how could God use someone to do what I have to do? God is good and loving and…who am I kidding… He could never use people to do what I have to do." He blurted out, almost rambling and then searched her face.

Cory held his gaze and answered without hesitation. "Of course, He could."

She doesn't get it, he rationalized to himself. *If she did, she'd tell me to leave and never come back. She deserves a godly man.* "I kill people!" he blurted out, his chin dropping to his chest in shame.

Almost relieved, Cory immediately saw his problem. It must have been an especially difficult and casualty-laden mission for him to struggle like this, but she knew exactly what he needed to hear—not her words, God's.

"Do you believe the Bible is true?" she asked.

Stunned, he looked up at her. "Did you not hear what I just said? I kill people. I know I told you I felt the military was where God had called me, but how could He call men to do what I sometimes have to do?"

"I know what you said, and I asked you a question. Do you believe the Bible is true?" she answered back, chin defiantly in the air.

"Sure. Why?" he replied, softening.

"Because you asked me a question, and I've learned that the Bible is the best place to go to find answers. If the Bible is true, then it can tell us if God could use men like you. Right?

"Yes" he answered hesitantly, intrigued.

"I happen to love the Old Testament. It's full of so many people, not superheroes, like some imagine, but real people like you and me. In recent years, I've been teaching the Old Testament a lot, and I have a new favorite character. This person shows up in Exodus. He is always with Moses. In fact, he keeps out of a lot of trouble because he loves God so much. You know the time when everyone tells Moses to put a veil on after being in God's presence because his face is glowing?"

"Yeah."

"Well, this guy wasn't afraid. In fact, the Bible says he would spend all day in the tabernacle in the presence of God. He wasn't afraid of a glowing face, he wanted to have one! I'd say that's pretty godly. Later, the Bible states that this man did everything God told Moses to do. Did you catch that? He did everything God told Moses. Moses didn't do it. This guy did. Then, at the end of his life, he states that his whole house will follow God, and they did—his whole house and all of Israel—all his life, all the lives of his men. All the way until his grandchildren's generation, Israel followed God. That is some kind of influence. He was a godly man. Don't you think so?"

"Yeah"

"Do you know who he was?" she asked, leaning in. "Joshua," she answered her own question. "Joshua. He's got his own book in the Bible. Know who I'm talking about?"

"Of course, I do." Realization of where she was headed began to dawn in his eyes.

"Wouldn't you say that Joshua was a godly man used by God for His purposes?" she asked.

"Yeah." A smile hinted at the edges of his eyes and mouth.

"Z, if you are struggling with whether or not God could call a man to military service, that's not God. That's Satan trying to trip you up. God is a God of love, but He is also just. You don't go out to kill for no reason. Sometimes, God brings *justice* Himself, but most often, He uses others to bring it. God commanded Joshua to go into the land and take it. He was instructed to kill them all—not because God is mean. Read the Scripture. Abraham wanted to kill the Amorites for what they had done to his nephew, but God told him he could not. God stayed the hand of Abraham in order to give those people a chance to turn to him, but four hundred years later, they had not, and justice had to be served for their sin. Through Joshua, God brought that justice. Through Babylon and Persia and Rome, God brought the same judgment on the Israelites. Who carried it out? Military men and women. We know Joshua was a godly man, and we know that he had to do some hard things in obedience to God. There have always been those God uses like that. Think about it. When you go, you are going to an area of the world where evil men kill innocents for sport. You put your life on the line to stop that evil. As you put your life between theirs and eternity, God can use you to open their hearts to him. He can use you to give them a chance. If you should have to take a bullet for them, you know where you will be going, and they will live to have the chance to join you there. Your courage and sacrifice can be God's tools. Who knows what He is doing in the Middle East right now because of men and women like you. He is a great big God, you know."

He sat, looking at her. The smile in his eyes now glinted with moisture. *There it is*, he thought. *I've known that all along, but I just never put it together. How many sleepless nights have I spent torturing myself over whether or not God could use me like this? I've wasted a lot of time flipping back and forth between surety and doubt, putting on a good "Christian" front to others while harboring doubts deep inside.*

"Thank You" was all he could manage audibly. With one fluid movement, he swung his leg over the bench and leaned on the table facing the sunset.

Not knowing what he was thinking but completely aware of the smile and tears, she mirrored his move, and the two sat side by side on the bench, fists propping up their chins, watching the sun set. Comfortably silent, the two watched the light show as God said goodnight with a beautiful display of gold, yellow, red, pink, and purple.

Ezekiel dropped his right hand to the table in front of him. Cory did the same with her left. Without looking her way, he reached over and took her hand. Without a word, the two sat holding hands, watching the world revolve from day to night. The sun peacefully giving way to the night sky seemed an outward display of the Son peacefully taking over the doubts inside a man whose heart longed to be as obvious a display of God's love and power as the sunset in front of him.

Cory couldn't help but feel that God was doing something inside Ezekiel. She prayed deep within that he would listen and find the comfort he needed. She prayed that the warmth once radiated by the sun from without would remain within them both as they sought to shine in an ever-darkening world.

After who knows how long, Ezekiel broke the silence. "Well, God has said goodnight with a beautiful sunset, so I had better as well."

Both rose, Z still holding her hand, and walked over to the motorcycle. He turned to face her.

Peering into her eyes, he spoke quietly. "I'm not really good with words, but I think you already know that God used you to help me tonight. Thank *you*, from the bottom of my heart. Thank you."

With a squeeze of her hand, he reached for his helmet and, in one fluid movement, was astride the motorcycle. Cory stepped back as he started the motor.

"I will be calling to set up that date," he pronounced as he rode down the driveway and out into the night.

Cory watched till she could see him no longer, then turned to head inside, a smile creeping across her lips. Boy, did she have something to write in her journal tonight!

Cory had fallen in love with Jesus as a child. She was raised in a loving home. Her father was a bivocational music/education minister. Her mother had been born with a disease and faced a lifetime of doctors telling her she couldn't. Instead, God had shown everyone she could. This was nowhere more impactful than in the very existence of Cory herself. When they got married, Cory's parents believed the doctors when they said it was physically impossible for her mother to have children. When she became pregnant, they immediately recommended abortion. That was out of the question, and to the doctors' amazement, she had an incredibly easy pregnancy and not only one but three girls. This led her parents to never let the girls forget that they were on this planet because God had a plan. The wisdom of science couldn't explain their existence, only God could.

Throughout Cory's life, she saw again and again in the lives of her parents that God was real, and loving Him drove you to give everything and trust fully. Their family never had a lot, and her mother's health issues meant day to day required a team effort. In the midst of all this, Cory was encouraged to ask questions and find answers in God's Word. Unlike a lot of minister's kids, Cory never desired to rebel or turn from Christ. In fact, on a mission trip to Shiprock, New Mexico, she was forced into teaching a class of preschoolers. She was petrified, but her father needed the help. There were just too many children at the VBS. So, she—at age 14—was responsible for introducing ten little ones to Christ. After the week's experience, at a celebration service back home, she knew God wanted to use her in a special way. She didn't know how. All she could think of was becoming a missionary in a far-off land or marrying a preacher. Neither seemed quite right, but she trusted that God only wanted her surrender, so she had.

The years that followed wouldn't be easy, but she would find herself with a bachelor's and master's degree in education. Her heart would be full as she taught teenagers about Christ. Oh, she taught in public school for a while, but God continued to place her in teaching positions in the church. She was keenly aware of the controversy this could cause and even more aware of what God's Word said about being a stumbling block. It seemed she found herself in areas where she walked the tightrope. While this seemed like a precarious situation to many, Cory realized that the delicateness required forced her to hold fast to God's Hand—and wasn't that where she needed to be?

In this way, God had led her throughout her life. She thought, like most girls, that she would marry and have children someday, but that was not to be. Many saw this single young woman working in small churches and encouraged her to go to bigger churches that "had something for her." That was code for men—the marrying kind. That had never been an option for Cory. She went to church to worship the God she loved, not look for a man to love. Her answer to the well-meaning sisters in Christ had been "If I am where God wants me to be, then He can find the man for me. If I stop looking for what God wants and start looking for a man, I'll just mess it up!" And so, here she was, almost fifty and still single. In her heart, she knew that this was God's plan. Looking back, she had no regrets and could see His hand guiding her to people and places that would have been impossible if she had been a wife and mother. No, she was where God wanted her. Right now, that was at a small country church full of precious loving people. Just as in times past, she found herself on staff. This time, it was leading music. She hadn't gone there to be the music minister; God had just placed her there, and now these sweet people were His conduit for loving on her. She loved teaching Sunday school to the young adults and leading the music. Never once did she go that she didn't leave knowing she had been with God, feeling that she was loved and needed.

This Wednesday was no different. She and her father went to church and stood around outside the auditorium, visiting with those who came early or waited outside while the kid's mission study went on. They solved most of the world's problems sitting out there laughing and sharing. When it was time, they moved into prayer meeting. After singing a few songs, the pastor shared a psalm, and they opened their prayer list. List was a misnomer. List implies a few names on a page. This was more of a prayer pamphlet. As they shared updates and added new names, Cory felt an urging in her spirit. She had a request. What? She felt God urging her to get these folks to pray with her, but for what. She racked her mind for what she hadn't already shared with them. Then, like a picture in her mind's eye, she saw those blue eyes. A smile spread across her face. Of course, these precious folks would pray.

"I've got a prayer request. I met a soldier the other day. He is in the Special Forces. He gets called out at random times when he is needed. His name is Ezekiel. I told him I would pray for him. Could we put him on the list?" Cory shared.

"Of course," exclaimed the pastor. "Our boys can never have too many praying for them. What was that name again?"

"Ezekiel. Ezekiel Christian."

"What a great name. Is he one?" an elderly woman in the back asked.

"As a matter of fact, he is. He is teaching a class for chaplains at the seminary," Cory responded,

"Well then, he's in combat whether he's overseas or not! They need godly chaplains," the pastor added.

Cory's heart felt warm. She knew these precious folks would pray, and God would hear. Oh, He always hears, but there's something special when his saints pray. And these saints will pray.

Sunday rolled around, and Cory was wrapping up her Sunday school lesson. How she loved talking about God with these precious young people. Unlike other churches, this group of "young people" were not teenagers. When Cory had come to this church, they had a children's program, a youth program, a men's and women's Sunday school, and an older couples' class. They had asked Cory to teach a class they called Adult 1. It was kind of a catch all for those who fit nowhere else. For a while, there were no people for the class, but one Thanksgiving, a recent graduate had asked if she came for Sunday school, would Cory be there. From that day on, a small group of twentysomethings had hungrily devoured God's word together in Sunday school class. How nice it had been to have a class that came because they wanted to talk about God. No teenage angst or drama, just glorying in the wonder of Who God is and how we fit in His plan. Closing with a prayer, they chatted as they headed into the sanctuary.

Cory stopped when she heard a voice she recognized. Oh, she recognized all the voices in this small church. There were only fifty members! This was a familiar voice she wasn't expecting to hear. As she rounded the corner and entered the worship area, she looked up, and there they were. Those eyes! Z stood there, talking with Cory's father and the pastor. With a giant smile, she politely excused herself from her classmates and headed toward the men.

"There she is." Her father greeted her. "Look who I found."

"Wow, I'm so glad you joined us this morning!" she greeted Ezekiel. "I see you've met our pastor."

"I sure have, and He is definitely a kindred spirit," he replied

The two older men excused themselves. Her father headed to the choir loft and the pastor to his post at the door greeting incoming worshippers.

"I hope it's okay that I invaded your spiritual family," Ezekiel began apologetically. "I just woke up this morning feeling that I needed the love of a downhome church. I remembered you talking about yours and knew I needed to be here."

"You came to the right place," she responded with a smile. "We don't have the biggest church or the most eloquent pastor or the flashiest music, but we know how to love and make people feel at home."

Just as she finished her sentence, an elderly woman approached. "Good morning, Cory! This wouldn't happen to be that soldier we're praying for, would it?" she beamed, taking him by the arm.

"It sure is," Cory affirmed.

"Well, son, I'm glad you're here. I love it when God gives me a face to go with a name for my prayer list. I must say, yours is a much more handsome face than I had imagined!" she said with a wink as she squeezed his arm, then moved down the aisle to her seat.

"Told ya." Cory giggled. "We don't try to be formal here. Everybody is family when they walk through those doors."

"You asked them to pray for me?" he asked.

"Of course. I added you to our prayer list on Wednesday. I hope that's okay," she said as concern crossed her face.

"Yea, it's more than okay," he quickly comforted. "I didn't mean to worry you. I appreciate it." He stumbled for words and scolded himself for being so clumsy. He thought to himself, *I'm just excited you care enough to ask them to pray.*

"Can I sit with you?" he verbalized.

"Umm—" she hesitated, thinking.

"If you don't want me to..." he broke in.

"No, I do want you to," she stumbled. "I just have to be up there until the song service is over." she continued, pointing toward the front. "I was just thinking about where I'll sit when I come down. You can sit, and I'll come join you. We come down for the sermon."

"Oh." He smiled, relieved. "That would be great. Where do you want me to sit?" I *should have known she would sing in the choir*, he scolded himself inwardly. *I must look stupid.*

Cory broke into his thoughts, "How about right here?"

"That's great." Ezekiel settled into the pew, and Cory gave him her things before heading to the stage.

Others began to file into the little church, and many came by to introduce themselves to Ezekiel. This was indeed what he needed. These genuine folks weren't trying to impress anybody or here because they were expected to be; this was a family.

Meanwhile, Cory was greeted with smiles and nods as she got to the choir loft.

"So is that your new man?" one woman teased.

"If he's not, I'll take him," said a little widow on the front row. The choir all laughed together.

"That is the soldier I told you about, if that's what you mean," Cory confirmed. With knowing smiles and a familiarity that only family has, they continued to tease and fellowship together until it was time for the service to start.

Cory had the choir stand, and they began to sing the call to worship. As they did, the folks in the congregation made their way to their seats, and the service was underway.

Ezekiel had been unaware that Cory was the minister of music. *Of course, she is*, he thought to himself. His thoughts went back to how she led the singing at the seminary party the night of their first date. I should have known. He joined in with the congregation as they sang an old hymn with the choir for the call to worship. When Cory encouraged them to pick up a hymnal, he felt transported to his early years. The songs they sang flowed from him as they had when he was young. This little congregation just sang from their hearts, and he too worshipped and sang melodies and harmonies that brought him back to a childlike faith he had forgotten.

The song service wound down, and the ushers brought the filled offering plates and laid them on the altar. Ezekiel bowed his head as the pianist played. He talked with God. He knew that he had been attending churches because the other professors expected him to be at those churches—you know, big ones. He hadn't just gone to worship in a long time. Perhaps his arrogance or desire to fit in had driven him to put God in a box and cruise on the history of his relationship with his Savior. He confessed to Jesus and asked God to speak to him during the remainder of the service, to speak to him vividly as He had in the past. He just wanted to know that God was still at work and had a plan for his future.

God must have let out a laugh and elbowed an angel as He said "Watch this" and answered Ezekiel's prayer.

Cory stood and walked to the podium as the pianist completed her offertory. The recorded strains of an accompaniment disk wafted from the speakers, and Cory began to sing. Ezekiel lifted his head as he heard the familiar song. She was singing a Southern Gospel song called "Written in Red."

"In letters of crimson, God wrote His love..." She sang. The song was a love song from Jesus to His children. As she sang the chorus, Ezekiel received the answer to his prayer. In a moment, he saw what he knew to be Jesus standing beside Cory. He looked around to see if anyone else saw what he saw. The people were worshipping along with Cory and seemed oblivious to Jesus standing there. Cory herself sang on, noticing nothing. He blinked, realizing he must be having a vision. Jesus reached toward His heart as if pulling something out. He held his closed fist out for Ezekiel to see. Slowly, Jesus opened his fist. There, in the palm of His hand, Ezekiel saw what he knew represented his own heart. He remembered asking God to hold his heart a long time ago. A smile spread across Jesus's face as Ezekiel demonstrated understanding.

Then, as if on cue, Cory—who was worshipping herself—held out her hand, palm to the sky. Jesus carefully placed Ezekiel's heart in her hand. Completely unaware of the vision, Cory closed her fist and pressed it against her chest at her heart. When she dropped her hand, Ezekiel looked back to Jesus. His hand was out again, fist extended. He slowly opened His hand again. There was what he understood to be Cory's heart. It slowly opened to reveal his heart inside. Then Jesus was gone.

Ezekiel closed his eyes. He had asked God to vividly speak to him about his future. He had wanted God to simply assure him that God had a plan. He never expected this! God was showing him that while God had been holding his heart all these years, it was time for him to give his heart to Cory, and in so doing, God would be holding both their hearts. God had never worked in his life like he worked in others, but this? Nothing like this had ever happened to him. He was a pretty traditional, conservative Christian. Weren't visions the kind of things Charismatics talked about? Not him.

"My ways are not your ways. For God's thoughts are higher than man's thoughts."

The words from Scripture sprang to his mind. He smiled, knowing that it was God's doing. He knew too that his future was firmly in God's hands.

Cory finished the song, and the congregation burst into worshipful applause. She walked from the podium to the pew where Ezekiel sat. She sat down next to him. He handed her Bible to her and mouthed "Beautiful" as they smiled at one another. She mouthed back, "Thanks." With that, the sermon began, and the down-home country preacher shared from his heart, and the people responded, laughing at his jokes, "amen"-ing his solid points and, finally, standing as he guided them into the invitation. Through it all, Ezekiel found himself in genuine worship as he had not done in a long time.

When the service was over, after being greeted by EVERYONE in the service, Cory and Ezekiel walked out to their vehicles.

"Cory," Ezekiel began, "would it be okay if I came back to your church?"

"Of course, it would." She beamed.

"I don't want to invade your space or anything, but I really felt at home today. I've visited everywhere, but nothing felt like home, until today," he explained.

"I know exactly what you mean. People are always telling me I should go to a bigger church where there is 'more for me,' but this church just feels like I belong. These precious people have made me feel needed and loved."

Come back he did. Ezekiel came that Sunday night and the next Wednesday, and on the following Sunday, he joined the church. He was welcomed with open arms and found himself growing ever closer to Christ. That affected everything. His classes at the seminary benefitted from his increasing relationship with God. His brothers in arms noticed a new vigor as they served together as well. He seemed to have a new hunger for God and his Word. As he grew, he held on to the vision he had experienced. He told no one but gloried in the fact that God was indeed at work in his life. God had heard his prayer and demonstrated it in an unexpectedly vivid way. He faced each day excited about what God might do next and determined to trust God and move in His timing.

His relationship with Cory was blossoming as well. The two were becoming great friends. They sang together at church often and found they loved sports as well. They spent many evenings with her father, watching all kinds of sporting events. Though he was sure God was leading the relationship with Cory, he was also aware that he had seen the vision, and Cory had not. He didn't want to scare her away. She seemed truly unaware of his feelings.

He was right. Cory had no idea. She just had no frame of reference for relationships with men. Besides that, she honestly felt that Ezekiel was too good-looking to be attracted to her. She made a concerted effort to remind herself that he must only care for her as a friend and to guard her heart against falling for him. She was pretty convinced that she was destined to be an old maid. She even joked that if she was Catholic, she would be a nun.

Through it all, God was indeed at work in both of them.

Cory and Z were heading home from a Texas Rangers baseball game. It had been an enjoyable, if not hot and muggy, evening, and the Rangers were on fire. They had cheered home runs and shouted for timely outs. All in all, it was a great day. As they headed home, the traffic was terrible. There must have been a concert at AT&T Stadium, where the Cowboys played next door to the Rangers Ballpark because it seemed everybody was trying to get home.

"Why don't you give your dad a call and tell him we're on our way so he won't worry about you," Z said as he pointed to his phone lying in the cup holder between them.

"That's a good idea," she said. She picked up the phone as if it was an alien life-form. She looked all over it for how to turn it on.

Z just laughed as he watched her out of the corner of his eye. Finally, she gave up.

"How do I turn this thing on?" she asked in desperation.

He took the phone and, without even looking, turned it on and hit a button that dialed the number for her. He handed it back to her. She awkwardly put it to her ear and, when her father answered, explained their situation. When she was finished, she put it back in the cup holder as if it was contagious.

Z laughed out loud and asked, "What is it with you and phones?"

Cory was quiet.

"Is it that bad?" he asked again, realizing that this was no joke.

"Well, it's bad for me," she replied. With some hesitation, she continued. "When I was teaching, I had a stalker." She let the word hang in the air. Z shot her a glance but said nothing. The look on her face as she stared out the front window clearly said that this was a big deal. She appeared to be struggling with whether or not to tell him. He deliberately kept his focus on the road so as not to pressure her one way or the other but secretly prayed she would tell him.

"I started getting notes in my mailbox," she began, deciding he deserved to know. After all, he had trusted her with his deep fears. She could trust him.

They would describe everything I had been wearing down to what earrings I had on. Then they would describe all kinds of things that never happened. At first, I thought it was some kind of prank by my students, but then, one day, I came home from school, and the phone was ringing. I quickly picked up the phone and an unfamiliar male voice began talking. I responded hesitantly, trying to figure out who the voice belonged to. If it was one of my students, I wanted to figure it out and put an end to this. But I didn't recognize it. This was not the cracking, changing voice of one of my middle schoolers. This was a deep man's voice. He talked as if we were best friends. He talked of how we had been to the movies and what a wonderful time we had. I was so stunned. I froze. When I finally got myself together, I hung up.

The next day, there was another note. I walked into my house, and the phone rang. Instinctively, I reached for it, but I froze. What if it was him? I waited and let the machine answer it. It was him. He began talking about seeing me that day. I was horrified. I had seen no one. As he droned on into the machine, I wracked my mind for any man that I had seen that day. I could think of no one. When I came out of my thoughts, I realized he was still talking to the tape. I reached over, picked up the phone, and set it back in the cradle, hanging up on him.

Day after day, this happened. I would hang it up, so he would call while I was at school and talk until the tape on the machine was full. It was awful. He went from his fantasy world of what we had done to what we were going to do. He told me all the things we would do together. I began to feel like I was being watched. I was.

My sister lived with me, and I would go nowhere without her. She became my security. I stopped walking home from school even though it was only a few blocks away. Soon, I began to feel his eyes on me all the time. After about three months, he revealed himself. I saw him watching me at one of my volleyball games. At first, I didn't know it was him, but then he was everywhere. Just standing there. Watching. He started going to my church. I shared with a couple who were friends of mine. They encouraged me to talk to the pastor. He just blew it off saying I was being too sensitive.

One day, there was a knock on the door. My sister answered the door while I was in the laundry room. I recognized his voice immediately. He pushed his way past my sister and sat on our couch. I ran out the back door and drove to our friends' house. They rushed to my house and made him leave. I felt awful for leaving my sister alone, but I was freaked. She has always been strong and bold and my protector, but she couldn't get him to leave. Our friend's husband made him leave. From that time on, I stopped seeing him, but the phone rang or the answering machine beeped every day, and I felt his eyes.

I stapled blankets to my windows. I booby trapped doors and windows in case someone tried to come in. Soon, my sister had to move back to Texas. I knew I couldn't stay in that house alone, so one night, my friends showed up at midnight, and in one trip, I moved to a new house across town. My new home had a separate garage that you entered from the alley in the back, so my car was never sitting in sight. It took him two weeks to find me.

My neighbor told me that while I was at school, a man had come by and tried all the doors and windows to see if they were locked. Her husband was the police dispatcher, so she had called him, and he began to send cars by to try to catch him. There were no such things as stalker laws, so since they didn't catch him at it, they couldn't do anything. He found my new number and started calling again. He started leaving me presents on my porch and sending me flowers to the school. I took everything and threw it in the front lawn. I wanted him to get the message.

Every time the phone rang, it seemed it was him. I stopped singing in the choir at church because he joined and sat behind me. I didn't want to leave the house because I knew he was there, even if I couldn't see him. One morning, after two years of this, I went out to my locked garage. I unlocked the door and turned on the light. There, under the windshield wiper of my car, was a folded piece of paper. I froze. I wracked my brain to remember if it had been there the night before when I parked.

It hadn't been.

How did it get there?

Was the door locked?

It was.

Fear gripped my entire body. My eyes darted around the garage. There seemed to be hiding places everywhere. Every dark corner loomed as a place where he might be hiding.

My fight-or-flight reflex kicked in, and I turned and ran. I ran straight to my friends' house down the street. The wife was still home. She saw my white panicked face and listened to my hysterical ramblings. She came with me back to the garage. She took the note and began to read it. Not out loud.

"Something has to be done! she said as she folded it back.

I never showed anyone the letters I had gotten except my sister, and I erased and threw away the answering machine tapes. No one really knew all that was happening. I carried it all. She now saw and was horrified. We took the note to the police. They couldn't do anything unless I could prove he had put it there and trespassed. I couldn't prove a thing.

She showed it to the pastor to see if he could talk to the man. He said we were overreacting.

The letter was full of graphic fantasy about what "we" were going to do on my birthday. I wanted to vomit when I finally read it. When my friends' husband read it, he took action.

That night, I moved out of my house and into the bedroom that was vacated by their eldest daughter when she graduated high school the year before. Anyone wanted to talk to me, they went through them. I was never alone. I never answered the phone.

My world shrank to a bedroom in someone else's house, with blankets stapled on the windows. I began to feel protected until, one night, about two in the morning, I was awakened by a blood-curdling scream. The whole house came to life. My friend's younger daughter was coming home from a lock-in at church, and she caught someone—a dark figure—trying to break in my window. She screamed, and he ran. You could still see the tool marks where he pried at the window.

That was it. I resigned my teaching job. At the same time, my mother broke her back, and my father had a heart attack, so I moved back home to take care of them—and to escape. For years after I moved home, I still stapled blankets to my windows. I couldn't sit in front of a window at night without feeling I was being watched. That was more than twenty years ago. I've overcome almost everything. I don't have blankets on my windows. I don't feel watched, but...every time the phone rings..." Her voice weakened and trailed off.

"Every time the phone rings, my heart freezes." She took a deep breath, fighting back tears. "I know it's not him, but that sound takes me back there in an instant." She grew quiet, head down in shame.

"I just hate phones," she spat in almost a whisper, with a heart-wrenching pain and finality.

Z let quietness hang in the air. He had no idea. He had seen no evidence of all that pain welled up inside. He instinctively felt a fierce anger, and desire to protect her grow inside of him. He wanted to reach out and wrap his arms around her and tell her that no one would ever harm her—he would see to that.

In the midst of his indignation, God pulled him up short. He realized that this explained so much. He knew, to win her heart, he had to move in her timing. He had to let her know he could be trusted. He needed to be her friend.

In that moment, he realized that if she never let down the walls she had built, he would still fight to be the man she could trust. Even if she never trusted him with her heart, he knew she had already won his. Even if she could never love him, he already loved her. He quietly prayed that God would comfort her, that God would enable him to be what she needed. He prayed for wisdom.

As he prayed, she sat. Having voiced all that drained her. She felt small and weak. She hadn't realized that it was still all so vivid. It was as if it had all been only yesterday.

Oh, God, she cried out in her spirit.

Those were the only words she could muster. She felt weak and small. She couldn't believe she had just told him all that. She felt embarrassed and ugly. As if every ounce of energy drained from her body, she dropped her hands to her side. She expected to feel the leather of the seat, but that's not where her hand landed. Surprised, she looked down at her hand.

As he prayed, Z had placed his hand on the seat next to him. He had opened it, palm up in entreaty to God as he prayed. Suddenly, he felt her hand fall in his. Instinctively, he wrapped his strong fingers around her hand. His big muscular hand enveloped hers. Without looking away from traffic, he willed every ounce of his strength to flow to her.

As she stared at her hand, she felt the warmth of his hand wrapping around hers. Her hand seemed small as she noticed the strength of his. The power of that hand completely hid her hand from view. Looking at his hand, she was reminded of Jesus's words, "You are in my hands, and I am in the Father's. No one can snatch you from the Father's hands."

Slowly, almost coinciding with the warmth moving from his hand to hers, she began to feel the strength of God filling her, reminding her that in her weakness, God would be strong.

He said not a word; he didn't even look her way. It wasn't a romantic embrace, in fact, she didn't even think of him. He was being a conduit for God. She felt the weight of those memories and the cold fear dissolving in the warmth now enveloping her hand. She never even realized how strong that deep hurt remained buried inside.

Without lifting her head, she closed her eyes and let the grace of God remove that fear and begin to heal that wound. Quietly, a tear slipped down her cheek.

When the cold salty drop fell from her face, it landed on his hand. He cut his eyes to glimpse her way. That strong woman who had boldly confronted him over his doubts about God's calling sat there, broken and vulnerable. How could any man pursue his own designs so blindly that he would leave a woman so paralyzed in fear and feeling so alone? He fought the anger rising in him and, instead, prayed that God would heal her and let her know how precious she truly was.

The two drove in silence, but all of heaven was abuzz with the activity of God as He listened to Z and ministered to Cory. When they finally pulled in the driveway, Z gave her hand a squeeze and forced her to meet his gaze. He said not a word.

She hesitantly looked in his eyes, trying to form an apology, but when her eyes met his, all need to speak vanished. Without words, he offered his support, and she received it. A smile spread across each face. She lost the need to explain or apologize and felt…safe.

Z opened his hand but left it lying on the seat of the car. Cory slowly opened hers, palm down to match his. She didn't want to let go of the warmth she felt, but as she looked at their hands, she knew she could. A much stronger hand was still holding her. She would be okay.

Lifting her hand from his, she met his eyes again and smiled. This time, the weakness was gone, and she quietly whispered, "Good night."

He nodded and smiled as she exited the car and headed for the house. Just before she walked in the door, she looked back. She was met by those strong blue eyes smiling back, waiting for her to be safely inside. She waved and vanished into the house.

Cory thought the rain would never end. It seemed to rain every day. She loved the rain, but the earth could hold no more, and the resulting floods were beginning to take their toll. She was standing at the back door when the phone rang. There was still a tinge, but definitely not like before. She didn't run to get it either. She listened to see who was calling.

"Cory, it's me. Sorry to call like this, but I've been called out again, and I need your help." It was Z

Quickly, she picked up the phone.

"I'm here. What do you need?" she asked.

"Well, I hate to ask, but I have to head out, and my parents are stranded near their house. Their truck has stalled, and I can't go help them."

When Cory picked up the phone, the answering machine hadn't disengaged. Cory's father was listening and replied, "We can go help if we can find them."

Cory looked at her dad. She knew he really liked Z. He never would have volunteered to help if he didn't. When he was younger, he volunteered all the time, but these days, not so much.

She smiled and responded, "Daddy says we can help. Can you tell me where they are?"

Quickly, he explained. She wrote down where they were, got their phone number (her dad had a cell phone), promised to pray for him, and said goodbye. When she hung up, she whispered a quick prayer and then read her notes to her father.

The two of them set out to find Z's parents. She'd never met them, though he talked about them a lot. She hadn't realized that they lived so close. After about a two-hour drive, they found themselves on a small two-lane country road. Cory wasn't sure about where they were, but her father was, and he seemed to have some kind of internal compass. He hated to go the same way twice, and ever since she was a kid, she would swear they were lost, but he would turn a corner and be exactly where they needed to be. As a child, she thought it was one of his super powers. Now, she knew better than to doubt him, so she kept driving.

They rounded a remote corner, and sure enough, there was a truck on the side of the road. They pulled over and got out.

"Hello?" Cory called. "Mr. and Mrs. Christian?"

A handsome elderly gentleman got out of the car. "Howdy, I'm Mr. Christian." He was just like a cowboy out of some old western. The wrinkles on his friendly face hinted at the many smiles and wisdom that had etched each one.

"You must be Cory" came a lilting voice from the other side of the car. A similarly handsome woman came around the truck smiling. She had those same blue eyes Cory adored in her son. "I'm so sorry to bother you!"

"I'm sorry you have had to be stuck here so long. We came as soon as Z called," Cory continued as she shook both their hands.

"Let's take a look and see if we can figure out what went wrong," Cory's father offered as he shook Z's dad's hand. "Bob."

"Jim."

The two disappeared under the hood.

Just then, the passenger door on the back seat opened, and a beautiful fifty-something woman stepped out. She, too, had the smile and those eyes. Confidently, she moved around the back of the truck.

"Well, it's about time we meet you!" she proclaimed. "I was beginning to think there didn't exist a woman who could interest my brother, but he hasn't stopped talking about you since you met. My name's Abigail."

"And you can call me Sarah," his mother offered.

"Do you think those two can figure it out?" Abigail asked.

"He's not as young as he used to be, but I haven't seen a vehicle yet that he couldn't eventually figure out," Cory responded.

"Then they must be two peas in a pod, and maybe together, they'll fix it." Sarah laughed.

About that time, another vehicle drove up. A beautiful blonde stepped out of the car. By the look on her face and the way she carried herself, she seemed familiar with the Christian family.

"Well, there you are! I wondered when I didn't find you at home. I called Ezekiel, and he told me you were stranded, so I came as fast as I could," she said with a lilting voice.

"That's okay, Cory and her father are here to help us," Abigail said with what Cory thought was a tinge of disdain.

"But Ezekiel sent me to help. I promised him I would. You know I will do anything for him, and he always depends on me for whatever he needs." She seemed to say that last sentence for Cory's benefit.

Sarah stepped between the woman and Cory. "I appreciate your offer, Shelly, but Cory and her father are better equipped to help us, and Ezekiel asked her first."

Abigail joined the conversation, and the three women seemed to argue. It was evident that Abigail did not like Shelly and Sarah didn't want her help and Shelly was determined to stake a claim on Ezekiel.

As they continued, Cory walked around to where the men stood under the hood of the truck. They were absorbed in their job, and though Cory couldn't understand what they were talking about, it was evident the "fix" wasn't so easy. As she looked up from the engine, a movement from the back seat caught her eye.

There in the back seat were two teenage boys. The look on their face was one of disgust as they surveyed the situation—the same look of disgust, exactly the same look. They were obviously twins.

Cory approached the two. "Hi guys."

They nodded in unison in response.

"Do you have any reception out here?" she asked, knowing that they didn't. After all, they would have been on their phones on Instagram, Snapchat, or something if they did. They were teenagers. That's what they do!

"No," one responded

"And I can't wait to get out of here!" the other finished.

"Well, if I could get us out of here faster, would you help me?" she asked.

They both lit up. "You better believe it!" they said together.

"Okay, help me move the stuff from ya'll's truck to mine. Then you can help me find my way to your grandparents' house, and we can unload it. Then you can stay while I drive back to get them. How about that?" she proposed.

"You bet!" They hopped out of the truck and moved to the bed.

Cory moved back around to where the adults were, all absorbed in their conversations.

"Excuse me," she said over their voices. "The boys and I are gonna move the load from your truck to mine and take it back to the house. They can help me unload, then I'll come back here and get the rest of you."

"Hey, that's not a bad idea. I'll ride with you and bring the jeep with the tools back for the guys to work with while you and the boys unload the truck at the house," Abigail offered.

"That would be fine if anyone could get the boys to do anything," Shelly quipped, trying to be funny. "You know how teenagers are!"

Cory pointed to the boys at the back of the truck who just waved and gave a "that's real funny" smile.

"Well, if you can get those boys away from their phones and ready to help, you truly are a miracle worker," Sarah quipped.

"I'll give you a ride, Mrs. Christian, after all, Ezekiel wanted me to help you," Shelly added.

"No, thanks, Shelly. Looks like Cory has everything under control. You can go home now. Thanks anyway." Sarah dismissed Shelly who turned in a huff and drove away.

Meanwhile, Cory and the boys—James and John—transferred the load from one truck to the other. As she did with just about everything when it came to teenagers, she found a way to make it fun, and the three laughed and talked as they worked. The boys completely forgot about their phones and worked without complaint.

"Well, I think she has the boys' approval," Abigail said to her mother. "I think Ezekiel is not the only male Christian who seems to like her."

Her mother nodded as the two joined in on the fun.

When Cory's truck was loaded, she, Abigail, and the boys piled in and headed for the house. When they got there, they were met by three large dogs barking suspiciously at the strange truck headed across the bridge. Cory slowed so as to make sure they stayed out from under the wheels. As she did, she surveyed the incredible bridge she was crossing. It was a wooden bridge that appeared to be handmade. Underneath, a good-sized stream flowed steadily on its way to who knows where. There were stately trees standing watch on both banks, offering a picturesque shade and giving the impression they were crossing a covered bridge. She could almost picture the two boys in the back seat standing by the rail with fishing poles, probing the depths beneath for the night's supper. The thought brought a smile to her face. Once across the bridge, she navigated through the driveway and over to the barn standing nearby. Abigail jumped out, greeted the dogs, went into the barn, got the jeep, and headed back out.

"You boys take care of Cory until we get back. Help her put the stuff away, then take her in the house so she can wash up," she instructed.

"We'll take care of her, Mom. Don't worry!" they responded, waving.

As she drove away, the boys got out and guided Cory into position to make unloading easier. Cory deftly backed up closer to a side door of the barn and parked the truck.

When Cory got out, the dogs left off sniffing the truck tires and headed to her.

"Hope you like dogs," James commented.

"That's Shadrach"—he pointed to a black lab—"Meshach (a golden retriever)."

"And Abednego (a large mix breed of some sort)," John informed her. "They're great guard dogs, but since you're with us, they won't hurt you. They just want to check you out."

"Yeah, but don't be offended if they aren't very friendly," James added. "It takes them a while to warm up to people."

Even before he finished speaking, Abednego jumped up, placing his paws on her shoulders in a kind of doggie hug. She laughed and pet him vigorously.

"If this is their idea of not being friendly, I'm afraid what friendly looks like!" she exclaimed, laughing. "Hey, Abednego, it's nice to meet you."

She set his feet on the ground as the other two began to compete for her attention. She greeted each in turn, making sure they got an equal amount of affection.

"Okay, you three, we have work to do. You better leave me alone for now." She only mildly scolded the dogs, and they reluctantly retuned to exploring the various strange smells they could find on her truck.

The trio went back to work unloading the truck.

When they finished, Cory noticed a basketball goal. She grabbed the ball lying on the ground and threw it at James. "You got game?" she asked.

He instinctively caught the ball with ease and smiled back at her. She knew they did. They had to be about six four and were definitely athletic. They must look an awful lot like what Z had looked when he was younger.

"You bet. How 'bout you, Shorty? You got game?" he responded.

"Yeah," she said. "I can lose to anyone in a game of HORSE" A smile spread across her face.

"You're on!" John replied, grabbing the ball and taking a shot.

As they played, they talked and laughed. Cory really was bad at horse, and before long, she was one letter away from defeat.

"Well, before I destroy you, tell me, how did you and Uncle Ezekiel meet?" James asked.

"Actually, we met at Kroger." She chuckled, remembering.

"I might have guessed it be some random place. You're not like some of the girls who come here chasing my uncle," John added.

James elbowed him. "What he means is..."

"What I mean is what I said. We like you. Those other girls are like..." He searched for a word.

"Shelly," James finished. "We don't like them."

"You seem much more..." Again, he searched for a word.

"Real," again James finished.

"Well, thank you. That's the nicest compliment I've had in a while," Cory said with genuine gratitude. "And I'm not here to chase Z."

"Z?" they asked in unison.

"I mean Ezekiel," she corrected.

"Is that what you call him?" James asked.

"Yea. That's my name for him," she explained. "It just kinda came out, and it fits."

"I like it," John replied. "Can we use it? Uncle Z. That's cool!"

"Sure, you can use it. He told me he always wanted a cool nickname."

About that time, the jeep pulled back in the yard. This time, with all the rest of the adults. The women hopped out, and the men drove over to the barn.

"I didn't bring the right tools!" Abigail explained. "So he brought us back to start supper while they fix the truck."

The two men seemed like long-lost friends, working together in the barn as Jim introduced Bob to the dogs, showed him around the place, climbed back in the jeep, and headed off to the disabled truck.

"I'm gonna get some supper," Sarah called as she headed to the house.

"Mom talked your Dad into staying for supper in return for helping with the car. I don't know, but I think she really didn't have to try that hard. Our fathers are kindred spirits," Abigail explained. Then she looked at her boys with a quizzical look on her face.

"Where are your phones?" she asked.

The boys looked around, then back at their mother. "They're in the truck," James answered.

"What? You mean you are not glued to your phones?" she taunted.

"No," John stated matter-of-factly. "We've been talking with Cory. We like her."

"Well, that's high praise." Abigail laughed. "Do you mind if I steal her away to get cleaned up in the house?"

"Sure, we were just gonna beat her at horse anyway," James quipped.

"Yeah, we'll just beat her another time," John added.

"Yeah, you will," Cory agreed. "Thanks for your help with the truck. I couldn't have done it without you."

They nodded and went back to the basketball hoop, while Cory and Abigail headed for the house.

It was a beautiful house. With only a little imagination, you could almost see the horses tied to the rails out front. There was a big front porch with a swing. The three dogs lounged lazily on the porch and the steps. It looked just like the farmhouses that must have graced these grounds back when Texas was young. Behind the barn, sitting to the right of the house, was a corral, and a few horses could be seen standing in the shade by a water trough. It really gave the feel of being in the Old West. It wasn't a log cabin, but it was obvious the occupants were proud of their Texas heritage and enjoyed a stereo-typical rural cowboy lifestyle.

The two women climbed the stairs and entered through the wide front entry with a simple screen door. Mounted above the rails of the porch was a metal triangle and a metal bar hanging from it that had obviously seen many a dinnertime roundup. Cory smiled as she pictured Sarah using it to call the family to dinner.

The inside of the house was exactly what she expected after seeing the outside. It continued the country theme but with a modern comfort flair. The large living room had a welcoming well-used fireplace, and it opened to a large kitchen and dining room. Sarah called to them from behind a low counter separating the dining room from the kitchen.

"There you are. I could use a little help in here if you get a minute."

"Sure, Mom, let us clean up first," Abigail responded as she nodded toward a hall exiting off the living room to the right. "The restroom is right through there."

She and Cory cleaned up and returned to the kitchen. Immediately, they jumped in getting supper together. Cory really enjoyed these two ladies. They laughed and chatted, and before they knew it, the sun was beginning to set.

"Where are those guys?" Sarah wondered aloud. "They sure have been gone a long time."

Abigail decided that she would take her car and go check on them. As she headed out the door, the jeep and the truck drove in the driveway.

"Here they come." She reported and took the opportunity to call to her boys still playing basketball near the barn. "I don't know what you did, Cory. But I think anyone who can get those boys off their phone and getting along needs to come around here more often. They're still out there playing, not a phone in sight."

"I still can't get over the fact that you got them out of the truck and helping you unload and reload and unload again all that stuff. I didn't think anyone could pry them away from their phones," Sarah added as she set the table.

"I really didn't do that much. I just noticed that weren't using their phones like normal and guessed right that they had no service. I told them that if they gave me a hand, I'd get them back home so they could get connected to the world again. It worked," Cory explained.

"Yeah, but when I came back, you had the truck unloaded, and you were playing ball! They didn't go back to their phones." Abigail returned to the dining room. "What's your secret?"

"No secret," laughed Cory. "I'm just a strange newcomer, and they had a lot of questions."

"I hope they weren't too nosey," Sarah chimed in.

"Not at all. They were great, and I got filled in on some of the scoop around here too!"

At that moment, the boys came bounding through the door, followed by the two elderly men. They were all visiting and joking with one another.

"There you are," Sarah called over the noise. "You guys get cleaned up so we can get some food in those bellies!" She walked into the living room, and the boys dutifully kissed their grandmother on the cheek as they headed to the kitchen to wash up. As her husband leaned down to do the same, she asked, "Did you get it fixed?"

"Well, thanks to Bob, we got it running," Jim answered. "I don't know what I would have done without him. He knew exactly what it was, and between the two of us, we got it done. It took a while, but we did it."

"Yeah, we don't move quite as fast as we used to," Bob added, and Jim pointed toward the hall bathroom. Both men headed in to get cleaned up.

Soon, everyone returned, and with Sarah's guidance, each one took their place around the table. After Jim led them to join hands and say grace, they began chatting and sharing the night away.

The company was so sweet that they didn't hear the wind begin to pick up outside. They were oblivious to the brush of branches against the window and the light patter of rain as a thunderstorm blew in. In this part of the country, the weather was extremely volatile this time of year. In fact, there had been record flooding in the area. This season, the weather was proving the old saying, "If you don't like the weather in Texas, wait a minute, and it will change."

Suddenly, the lights flickered, and there was a loud boom from outside. Everyone froze, and there was silence in the house for the first time that night.

"Were we supposed to have storms tonight?" James broke the silence.

"We were stuck by the truck and didn't have our phones all day. How could we have known? John responded.

There was another loud boom, and the windows lit up with the lightning outside. In what seemed no time at all, the light patter of rain had turned into driving torrents, smashing against the walls of the house. Jim went to the window for a look.

"Wow, it's really bad out there." As he closed the shutters on the windows and signaled for the boys to do the same, he continued, "I think we're gonna get a lot of water tonight. I hope the creek doesn't flood. Bob, you and Cory might get stuck here!"

As he finished speaking, James and John put their hats on and headed out into the stormy night.

"Maybe it will be a quick one," Bob chimed in. "Sometimes, these things blow over as fast as they blow in."

The boys returned, flanked by the three dogs who took their places in front of the fireplace. James had rain splotches on his shirt and was brushing debris off his shoulder and fluffing his hair. They reported that all the windows were securely shuttered and the horses tucked safely in the barn.

Sarah hustled everyone into the living room. She and Abigail cleared the table and washed up the dishes while the men chatted pleasantly in recliners. The boys had grabbed Cory, and the three were sitting on the floor, watching a baseball game on TV and sharing their own expert commentary on what was happening. All in all, it seemed the storm outside couldn't dampen the fellowship that was taking place inside.

What the storm was doing was filling up the already rain-soaked ground around the creek. It only took a few minutes of the driving rain to coax the once gently flowing river out of its banks and over the bridge to the property. Unbeknownst to the happy crowd inside, they were being isolated from the rest of the world. That bridge was the only way in or out. The creek encircled the property, and though it wound for miles like a snaky fence, it effectively prevented any vehicles from crossing to the outside. Cory and Bob were now stuck.

Before long, Abigail rose from the counter where she and Sarah were pleasantly chatting.

"I hate to be the bearer of bad news, but you boys have baseball practice in the morning, and we should be heading home."

Reluctantly, the boys rose from their prone position on the floor, playfully complaining but gathering their things to leave.

"Aw, Mom," whined James. "The game's not over."

"Yeah, it would be rude to leave our guests," tried John.

Abigail just gave them her best "Mom" look, and the two willingly complied.

"We should be getting home too," said Bob as he rose from his recliner.

"No need to hurry off," said Jim. "That storm has died down, but it might let up soon and make for a better ride home."

"Well," said Bob, "this old man turns into a pumpkin when it starts gettin' too late. Cory better get me home before that happens."

He and Jim shook hands and headed for the door. While Cory said her goodbyes, the two boys headed out the door followed by the dogs, and the two men tarried on the porch still amiably chatting.

Cory smiled as she saw the men. Her father wasn't usually a talkative fellow, but it seemed he and Mr. Christian had really hit it off. She whispered a quick prayer of thanks to God for sending her daddy someone she was pretty sure would become a friend. The fact that he had stayed as long as he did was evidence of that.

Sarah must have noticed Cory and understood what she was thinking because she drew near and placed her hand on the younger woman's shoulder and whispered, "I've never seen my husband talk so much with anyone but family. I am so glad Ezekiel asked you two to come to our rescue. I'm never glad when he gets called out, but since it meant we got to meet you two, it's not so bad. I hope you two won't be strangers."

The two women embraced as they, too, headed out the door and on to the porch.

It was still raining. The wind had died down, so it wasn't a driving rain, but it was definitely more than a sprinkle. James and John had ventured out in it to bring their mother's car up to the porch.

From the darkness, there came a commotion. The dogs could be heard barking at something. The group on the porch was expecting to see Abigail's car pull up. Instead, the two boys came running back. The dogs circled and barked in front of Jim as if trying to send him a message.

"Pops!" James shouted. "You better come take a look at this."

"I think we have a problem," added John.

"What in the world is wrong, boys?" Sarah asked as Jim headed in to grab his hat and coat.

"Well, I was getting Mom's car when I heard what I thought was the wind. I realized the wind wasn't really blowing, so I tried to figure out where it was coming from. It's coming from the bridge, Granny," James explained.

"Oh, no," lamented Abigail. "Do you think the creek has overflowed?"

"I don't know, Mom. It's too dark to see."

About that time, Jim returned, handed a cowboy hat, flashlight, and raincoat to Bob, and the two men headed out with the boys and dogs to check things out.

It didn't take long for them to return. They were drenched from head to toe.

"Well, we got some bad news," Jim said as he mounted the porch. Cory couldn't help but grin as she listened to the slow drawl of his speech. There was just the hint of an accent that seemed to blend his Texas roots and time in Australia. He was the perfect picture of an old cowboy. He took his hat off to drain the water from its brim. "The bridge is washed out. There's no getting out tonight."

"Isn't there another way off the ranch?" Cory queried.

"I'm afraid not," Abigail said flatly. "Looks like we're stuck here tonight."

"She's right. That creek completely cuts this place off from the outside world. It's both a blessing and a curse. This would be the curse part," Sarah explained.

"Bob and I and the boys can try to fix the bridge, but that'll have to wait till the mornin' when we can see what we're doing. Let's just pray that water goes down while we sleep," Jim offered.

"Give me a minute, and I'll get a place fixed up for everyone," Sarah said as she headed inside.

"I'll give you a hand," Abigail chimed in as she followed her mother inside.

"Me too!" Cory offered.

As the three ladies gathered sleeping bags and pillows and blankets and arranged the sleeping situation, the fellas did their best to dry off. It didn't take long before Sarah gathered everyone together and gave out the sleeping assignments. Abigail and the boys would share her old room, while Bob and Cory would share Ezekiel's old room which had a bed and a pull-out couch. With the assignments all made, everyone began to make preparations to go to bed.

"Mom, can we stay up and watch the end of the game?" John asked.

"I don't want you bothering our guests," she discouraged.

"Oh, don't worry about me," Bob inserted. "Besides, Cory is a night owl, and she would probably love to stay up and watch it with them." He winked at the boys, and they whispered thanks back at him.

Seeing the exchange, Abigail relented, smiling. "All right. Just try to be gracious hosts okay? I don't want to wake up in the morning and have to apologize for you guys being rude."

With that, the group split up. As Cory and the boys made themselves comfortable to watch the end of the game, the others headed off to bed. The trio in the living room quietly cheered and high-fived as they watched their team play. Before too long, though, even they surrendered to the strain of the day and fell asleep.

Cory was indeed a night owl, and as the boys snoozed in the recliner, she found herself going in and out of sleep on the couch. She loved a good storm, and the rain seemed to dance musically off the roof of this old house. That, along with the creaks and moans of a house that had seen many other stormy nights, created a symphony that drew her to listen. As she found herself more awake, she began to pray. She didn't have her Bible and journal, but that couldn't stop her from spending time with her Lord. Quietly, she reviewed the day with God and thanked Him for this precious family. She thanked him for her father's new friend, and she prayed for a blessing on all of them.

She had just begun to pray for Z's safety when she heard a noise that got her attention. All the noises were strange because this was an unfamiliar place, but there was something about this noise that gave her pause. She froze on the couch and strained to discern what exactly it was.

She heard nothing. Soon, she let herself relax and began to pray again for the soldiers who served with Z.

There it was again. Was that a footstep? Was it a creaking board? Maybe something had blown up on the porch. She tried to focus on the area near the door. It was dark, but the intermittent flashing of lightning offered glimpses of the area. As she stared toward the door, she thought she saw the doorknob turn. Her heart froze.

Quietly, the door was pushed open.

Cory couldn't move as fear gripped her. *Oh, God, help*, she cried out in her heart to the only help she had. She tried with all her might to melt into the couch so she wouldn't be noticed. Time seemed to stand still.

The figure turned and, with great care, closed the door so as to keep it from making any noise.

The dogs, Cory thought. *Where are the dogs?*

A quick flash of light revealed that they were asleep—one at each recliner, and Abednego at the foot of the couch. For a moment, she whispered a thank you to God as she gently shook Abednego with her foot.

She was sure he would wake up and attack the person at the door, waking the other dogs. She calculated that they would wake the rest of the house and give her and the boys a chance to get to safety.

Abednego did wake up.

But he didn't alert.

Instead, he began to wiggle all over.

What was happening? The boys said these were guard dogs?

As fear began to battle with common sense, Cory searched her mind for an interpretation for what was happening.

An especially bright flash of lightning aided her.

As the lightning lit the room, she could see Abednego had tackled the figure almost silently and was excitedly licking it.

Cory's fear began to ebb as she realized that whoever this was belonged here. Abednego obviously knew them. Still she did her best to remain hidden—just in case.

A soft giggle could be heard coming from the pile on the floor. Soon, the two other dogs had joined the wriggling slobbery mess.

"Shhh." She heard the figure say. "We don't want to wake the boys."

Instantly, Cory recognized the voice. All fear drained away as all the puzzle pieces fit, and the situation came clearly into focus. Still, she remained quiet.

"Come on, boys, let's go in my room and let them sleep."

"You do, and an old marine is liable to give you the fight of your life," Cory said softly. She watched as Z first froze, then frantically searched the darkness.

"Cory?" he spoke to the darkness. "What are you doing here? Where are you?"

Quickly, smoothing her hair, wiping under her eyes to remove any stray makeup and biting her lips to add a little color, she sat up on the couch. "Over here."

Z moved through the throbbing mass of dog and over to the couch. He repeated himself, "What are you doing here?"

Cory moved the blanket and patted the couch next to her. Abednego immediately jumped up and placed his head on her knee. Instinctively, she scratched him between the ears. As he sat, Z joined the scratching as Abednego happily thumped his tail, and the other two returned to their spots near the recliners.

"Looks like you have a new friend," he said in just above a whisper.

She found the smile now spreading across his face to be enchanting, and she responded with a warm smile of her own.

"Well, as you must have noticed, the bridge washed out, and Daddy and I are stuck. What are you doing here?" she asked.

"We were told to stand down. I guess our window of opportunity closed," he responded with a weird flatness to his tone.

Cory noticed the tone and his averted gaze and decided that line of questions wasn't wise, so keeping a light tone, she altered the question.

"I guess that explains why you're not with your unit, but I was really asking how you got here. The bridge is out," she clarified.

"Oh, yeah, well"—he puffed up his chest—"I'm special forces…'Neither rain, nor sleet, nor dark of night—'"

Cory interrupted, "That's the postal service motto."

"Right. Well, I used my mad ninja skills, tied a rope to a tree, and Tarzaned across the water, if you must know," he confessed.

"I'd think you'd want me to know about that. That's pretty impressive!" she responded, "Did you give a yell as you swung across?"

"My yell could rival Carol Burnett," he teased.

Wanting him to feel comfortable, she continued steering the conversation away from his day's events.

"Well, I'll have you know you just about scared me to death"—she grabbed two handfuls of Abednego's hair—"and this guy didn't help at all!"

Abednego promptly rolled over to expose his belly.

"Yeah, these guys are so ferocious."

"So I see." She laughed.

"They really are good watchdogs, but I guess they have the same weakness for you that I have."

She smiled, feeling him relax and kept the safe conversation going.

"Well, you should have seen our dads out there working on that truck. They were in hog heaven. I couldn't believe it when Daddy took your mom up on her offer for supper. He's usually ready to head home. Then the storm snuck up on us."

He listened as she related the events of the day. He knew what she was doing, and he loved her for it. She had picked up on his hesitation talking about the mission, maybe even suspected he was not exactly honest, and she seamlessly switched gears. She didn't pry or try to "fix" him. She respected him and moved on.

"And so, the boys and I fell asleep watching the end of the game," she finished. His smile had changed as she rattled on. "What?"

"Thank you," he whispered.

"For what?" she asked.

"For not grilling me about where I was today."

Cory turned her body to face him and looked him square in the eye.

"Listen to me. I will always want to know everything about you, but I also know that, sometimes, you can't tell me. Please know, no matter how bad you think it is, if you need to talk, I'll listen. I want to listen. But if you can't talk, I won't be offended, and I won't ask. Nothing you say or don't say will change my opinion of you. I have seen with my own eyes and felt in my spirit that you are a man after God's heart, seeking to do what He's called you to do. If you need my help to help bear your burden, I'm here. If you must bear it alone, I trust you."

She saw tears forming in his eyes and wanted him to be able to process what she'd said.

"With that, I'll bid you good night." She rose and headed toward the room his mom had prepared for her and her father.

"Cory," he called after her.

She stopped and turned.

"Thanks. You can stay here on the couch. I'll sleep on the floor," he offered.

Cory smiled. "No, my momma taught me a verse that has protected me over and over. First Thessalonians says 'avoid the very appearance of evil.' I should sleep in the room with Daddy."

"Your mother must have been an incredible woman," he offered. "And who can argue when Mother and the Bible agree? Goodnight."

"Goodnight."

She woke to the pleasant sounds of a country morning. Birds were singing, bees were buzzing, a horse whinnied, and somewhere in the distance, she heard a calf hungrily bawling for its mother. Glancing over, she could see that her father had already tidied up his side of the room and was out. Slowly, she rose from her bed in the pull-out couch and began cleaning the room. Her father was a stickler for things like that, so his side of the room looked untouched. She, however, had a tendency to create a tornado around her, taking note of where things fell and trusting "later" with the pick-up. As she straightened, she looked around the room. There were no sports trophies or memorabilia left over from boyhood. It had a definite masculine feel but was rather sparse. The pictures on the wall were obviously real places, and her guess was Australia. She wondered if they were from where he grew up. On the shelves were neatly stacked books. She began to peruse them. Other than a few beautiful leather-bound Louis L'amour western novels, the rest were various translations, paraphrases, and version of the Bible: parallel Bibles, topical Bibles, study Bibles. It was obvious he spent a lot of time reading God's Word. She felt a warming in her heart. Scattered randomly throughout the Bibles were books by EM Bounds and CS Lewis and Josh McDowell, books on prayer and apologetics. She hadn't really thought about what would be in his room, but this seemed exactly what she would have expected, simple, functional, and centered on Christ.

Cory was drawn from her reverie by the sounds coming from downstairs. She quickly finished cleaning, took a quick look in the mirror and did her best to erase the results of a night's sleep on her hair and make-up. After doing the best she could, she whispered a quick prayer.

"Oh, God, thank You for loving me no matter how I look. Help everyone else see me as You see me and may they see You in me and find that *beautiful*."

With that said, she headed out the door.

As she headed down the hall, she could hear talking coming from the kitchen, so she headed there. Sarah and Abigail were sitting at the table, drinking tea and chatting. Cory joined them at the table.

"Good morning!" Abigail greeted her.

"Good morning," replied Cory.

"Did you sleep okay?" Sarah asked as she pulled out a chair next to her. "Would you like something for breakfast? Coffee?"

"If you'll point me to the glasses, I'll just pour myself a glass of water," Cory replied.

Sarah pointed to a cabinet. Cory fixed a glass, and the three settled in for a chat.

"Are you sure you wouldn't like something?" Sarah questioned again.

"I'm not much of a morning person, so I usually sleep through breakfast. I'm really okay without anything," Cory explained. "I noticed Daddy was already up, but I don't see him."

"Yeah, the fellas got an early start on the bridge. Boy, was I surprised to find Ezekiel on the couch in the living room with the boys!" Abigail replied. "In fact, I don't think I've seen Ezekiel asleep since high school!"

"It has been a while since he's been able to sleep for very long periods. I think it's a part of his experiences overseas. He's always on the alert. It seems the smallest things would wake him with a start. This morning, I was able to cook breakfast for him before he awoke. I think God has been working on him," Sarah narrated.

"His sleeping isn't the only thing getting better. It seems since he met you he's more like the Ezekiel I grew up with," Abigail added.

Cory blushed. "I don't know about that."

"I do," Sarah jumped in. "He told me how you pointed him to Joshua to deal with his doubts. You helped him in a way none of us did."

"You would have helped him, given the chance. I'm just glad God could use me," Cory said. "What was he like as a kid?"

The women began to swap Ezekiel stories from his days growing up. Cory was glad for the subject change. She was beginning to feel a bit uncomfortable. Now, with the eyes off of her, she was gaining all kinds of insight and ammunition on Ezekiel. They laughed and fellowshipped for hours.

As lunchtime neared, Sarah made her way to the kitchen.

"Ladies, I think we need to take those hardworking fellas something to eat," she said.

The three of them packed up a picnic lunch. As they did so, Abigail spoke up.

"I have an idea. Cory, do you ride horses?"

"I haven't in a long time. I'm usually too heavy for trail rides," Cory admitted ashamedly

Abigail scoffed, "That's nonsense. We've got big strong working horses, and if you want to, I think it'd be fun to ride out to the guys."

"Well, I used to love to ride. I just don't want to hurt the horses. If you think it's okay, I'd love to ride again," Cory confessed.

Abigail headed out to the barn.

Sarah, sensing Cory's discomfort talking about her weight, walked over and put her hand on her shoulder.

"Come here, I want to show you something." She led Cory into her bedroom. "This is my family."

In the picture hanging on the wall, Cory saw a family of all different sizes and shapes. Sarah pointed to and described each one but never once did she use an adjective pertaining to their physical appearance. Finally, she pointed Cory to a picture of her young family with what Cory assumed were Aborigines.

"This is our Australian family." Again, she began describing each one. Cory noticed that all the aboriginal people were bigger than she expected. Even the Christians seemed bigger.

"Cory, I don't mean to pry, but I sensed some shame when you mentioned your weight earlier. I want you to know that we love people of all shapes and sizes. We don't love them because of the size of their bodies. We love them because of the size of their heart. You'll find this family doesn't see as most people see. I'm not just humoring you when I say that. I honestly never noticed your weight. You have made my son himself again, and my whole family has fallen for you and your father."

Cory had always been the big girl. She had been very athletic but, often, felt self-conscious that she wasn't thinner. In fact, that was part of her hesitation toward Z. She just felt he needed or deserved someone who was beautiful inside and out. He was so amazing to her that she couldn't see him thinking of her romantically. As she listened to Sarah, she remembered her prayer this morning.

"Help everyone see me as you see me..."

God was answering through Sarah, and that made Cory love her even more for it. She hugged the precious woman and whispered a sincere "Thank you."

Just then, Abigail beckoned from the front yard. The ladies grabbed the picnic baskets, mounted up, and rode toward the washed-out bridge.

It really was like riding a bike. Cory settled naturally into the saddle and immediately felt at ease. She rode atop a beautiful bay. She loved the feeling of freedom and couldn't help imagining what it must have been like to be a cowboy living out of a saddle. She took a deep breath. She loved the fresh air and the hint of a sweaty horse and saddle leather. The beautiful landscape surrounding her, the powerful animal beneath her, and the precious women beside her left her in awe of God's creativity. How could anyone believe all this was an accident? Nothing but an incredibly awesome God could have planned all this. She relished in the moment as they rode toward the bridge.

As the bridge came into view, the women could see the damage done. There must have been an incredible amount of water rushing down the creek to have taken out the bridge in the first place. There was debris scattered on both banks. The water was still flowing swiftly, but it was back within the banks. It was obvious the men had been hard at work, but the bridge was still undone.

Cory looked around for the men. She spotted her father and the boys near the back of a truck. They were measuring some wood. The smiles on their faces warmed her heart.

"Look who decided to show up." Jim cheerily walked toward the approaching ladies.

"We thought you boys might be getting hungry," Sarah answered as Cory and Abigail lifted the picnic baskets as proof.

"Did someone say food?" John alerted.

"Do I smell food?" James queried.

"I should have known you two boys would be ready to eat. You're always ready to eat!" Abigail laughed.

"They're not the only ones. I'm hungry enough to eat a horse!" Z stepped out from the bank of the creek and took Cory's horse by the nose. "Don't worry, Thunder. I'd never do anything to hurt you." He kissed the horse on the nose and continued whispering to her.

Cory couldn't help but stare. Z stood there shirtless, nose to nose with her horse. She had known he was athletic, but she wasn't prepared for how muscular he truly was. *It made complete sense. He was a soldier*, she told herself. Again, she found herself in awe of God's magnificent creations.

"Give us a hand, and we'll set up lunch while you guys clean up," Sarah called as Jim walked over and lifted her to the ground.

James did the same for Abigail. John and Bob began cleaning up the tools and placing the supplies in the back of the truck.

Z stepped from the nose of the horse to its side and reached up to help Cory dismount. She felt a moment's panic. He perceptibly caught it.

"Don't worry, I got ya," he encouraged.

"Are you sure?" she asked self-consciously. "I can get down myself."

"I got ya." He lifted her from the saddle as she placed her hands on his shoulders. Slowly, he lowered her toward the ground but stopped just short.

"Don't be scared," he said softly as he looked deeply in her eyes and saw an unfamiliar fear.

Cory realized she couldn't hide her discomfort from him. She met his eye and saw the genuine concern there.

Without breaking his gaze, she confessed, "It's just that we big girls aren't used to being off the ground. I'm really heavy, and I don't want to hurt you."

Intentionally, he held her off the ground as a smile spread across his face. "You aren't heavy to me. If you haven't noticed, I'm a pretty big guy. I've got you. Just relax and trust me."

She found herself peering deeply in his eyes. The strength she saw there made her begin to relax. There was no strain on his face at all, and he held her gaze quietly, willing her to trust him.

"Cory, bring me your basket. I've got the blanket spread, and I'm ready for the sandwiches," Sarah beckoned.

She broke his gaze and called over her shoulder, "Coming."

Looking back, she smiled at him warmly. Gently he placed her on the ground and unloaded the basket from the horse.

Handing the basket to her, he said, "I'll take care of Thunder. You better go help Mom."

She watched him walk the horse to the creek for a drink and tie him off before stooping to wash his face and hands. She turned and walked over to Sarah to help her get ready.

"Everything okay?" Sarah asked with a twinkle in her eye.

"Just fine." Cory smiled back.

The ladies set up lunch while the men cleaned up and took care of the horses. Once done, they joined together and sat around on the ground and the back of the truck, eating and chatting in the shade. It was a beautiful scene—the creek swiftly flowing and gurgling in the background, the wind blowing gently in the trees, the lilting sounds of birds and laughter floating on that breeze.

Soon everyone was done, and Jim spoke up.

"Well, I don't know about you young'ins, but my body is telling me it's time for a nap. I know you're probably in a hurry to get home, Bob, but we need to rest."

"I'm feeling what you're saying," Bob responded. "I do want to get home, but we're not spring chickens, and if we keep pushing, there'll be no going home. I'm with you."

"We'll finish up the bridge, Pops," John offered.

"Yeah, we can do it," James added.

"I know you can, but it's going to get really hot, and even you youngsters can get heat stroke. I think we need to break off for now." Jim ended the discussion.

"Hey, sis," Z called. "Could I use your horse and take Cory on a ride to see the place? That is if you want to go for a ride."

"I'd love to ride some more," Cory replied.

"Hey, if you want, feel free. I'll drive the boys back in your jeep.

"I'll ride Granny's horse back," John offered.

"Sure," Sarah smiled. "I'll ride back with these two old guys. See you at the house."

John immediately jumped on the horse and galloped back toward the house. Once he was out of sight, James asked, "Mom, can I drive back?"

Abigail looked at her younger twin. "How could I say no to that face?"

"Let us get out of the way first!" Jim laughed as they loaded up and drove back.

Once everyone was headed back to the house, Z and Cory strolled over to where the horses were tied near the creek.

"This really is a wonderful place. I think you'll be interested in some of the history it has to offer," Z explained as he helped her up on the horse and then mounted his own.

"History?"

"Yes, there is a wonderful old church house on the back forty. The foundation stone says it was built in the 1850s. We've always kept it. Not perfect—it needs a paint job and some dusting—but it's not falling down. I've spent many a day working out my aggressions and fears replacing rotting boards or contemplating the history of the place."

"Really?" Cory exclaimed. "I love that kind of stuff. Please, take me there!"

Z smiled knowingly as he led her there. The two chatted easily about the surrounding land and scenery. He took her along the creek.

"I wanted to show you this place first. It is one of the first places I discovered when we moved here." he narrated as they headed toward a stand of trees.

He stopped his horse and signaled to dismount. He took the reins from her and wrapped them around a branch. Looking at the stand of trees, Cory was confused.

Z smiled at the look of confusion. "Trust me. You can't see it yet, but this is a special place." He took her hand and led her around to where a branch seemed to lay over the tree next to it.

Grabbing the branch, he lifted it and directed her underneath it. As she followed his lead, she realized the branch was hiding a path. She followed the path, and the stand of trees opened to a small clearing. It was completely over grown by the trees, and the creek cut across the edge of the flat space.

"Wow," Cory responded. "This is like a great little fort hidden here in the trees. I can almost imagine an outlaw or an Indian taking shelter here."

He couldn't help but smile at her imagination. "You haven't seen the best part yet." He walked over to an area where a single ray of sun cut through the canopy of leaves above.

"I remember when I found this spot. It was really hot, and I prayed for God to help me find relief. I was able to sit in the shade and sip on the cool water. While I sat here drinking in the relief, I realized how like God this was. Right in front of me had been the very thing I desired, but focusing on my complaint, I hadn't seen it. When I cried out to God and began to look at things from His perspective, He helped me see what others didn't. I remember sitting here, pondering that fact, when I noticed this ray of light." He directed her attention to a ray of light that was streaming through the branches and leaves as if spotlighting something on the ground.

"It was as if God wanted me to see something. I thought, okay, God, what do you want me to see? I got up and looked over here."

He pointed to the ground and motioned for her to come look.

Cory moved to his side and looked down. Her eyes scanned the ground that seemed to be covered by fallen leaves and debris. Suddenly, something caught her eye. It was a flash of red. There, in the area where the light fell. Curiosity kicked in, and she bent to move leaves out of the way. Underneath the foliage was a beautiful red flower. It wasn't a rose but some beautiful little wildflower flourishing there in that one ray of light.

"God brought to my mind a couple of passages in Scripture as I looked at the little flower. The first one talks about the flowers of the field being taken care of by God. I thought, He created this wonderful space and put exactly the right amount of space between those leaves so that sun would shine through to allow this delicate little flower to grow. If He did all that for a simple flower, He must be doing something for me too." His face softened as he talked. "The other verse I thought of was where he told Samuel that we don't see things the way He sees them. I could easily have never known this flower was here. I could have only seen the outside twist of branches and missed the delicate beauty inside. I determined then that I wanted to see the world through God's eyes. I didn't want to miss the beauty hiding around me."

Cory couldn't help but smile. What a perfect living parable.

"I still come here and check on this little flower—especially when I begin to think there is no more beauty in this dark world. God has never let me down. Year after year, it's still here. And I never would have found it on my own. God"—he pointed to the light shining through—"had to highlight it for me."

Cory stood a moment and soaked in the profound example God had shown him. She knew God had led him to share it with her.

"Thank you," she said almost reverently.

He looked curiously at her. "For what?" he asked.

"For showing me this. I think I miss far too much focusing on my own complaints. I don't always realize the beauty that is right in front of me."

He smiled as he watched her look at the ray of light and the red flower. He couldn't help but think how she was a lot like that flower.

"Come on." He short-circuited the flow of his thoughts. "I want to show you some more."

They exited the hidden spot, mounted the horses and, once again, set off.

This time, Z guided them through the trees and up a path away from the creek. Soon, they found themselves on the edge of a small rise. They had climbed rapidly up, and there in front of them was a cliff.

Again, Z steered his horse to a nearby tree, dismounted, and tied him off. Cory did the same. As she did so, Z moved to the edge of the cliff and motioned for Cory to join him. He pointed to the view in front of them. The panorama view was beautiful. From here, you could see the creek meander on its way, the surrounding farms and ranches, and the road that led the way back to civilization. It hadn't seemed that the area was so full of rolling hills, but from this vantage point, they were clearly evident.

"I come up here and think of the psalm—" Z began.

"'I lift my eyes unto the hills...'" Cory broke in, smiling.

"'From whence cometh my help. My help comes from the Lord.'" They finished together.

"I just love to look out over the landscape. There is even a bald eagle that lives out here somewhere. Sometimes, he'll fly by, and I am just in awe of God," he shared.

It truly was a beautiful vista. "It makes me think of all the possibilities that could be out there," Cory commented.

"Me, too. I come here when I need to renew my hope for God's plan in my life," he shared as he scanned the landscape. As he did so, he couldn't help but wonder at how comfortable he felt sharing all this with her. He was generally so private and had never even told his family about these places, but as they continued, he was more convinced than ever that he could and should share this with her.

"Come on, we're not done yet," he said as he moved back to the horses. They remounted and followed the path back down. Soon, they emerged from the path and trees and moved away from the creek.

It wasn't long before the steeple appeared on the horizon.

"There it is!" Cory shouted excitedly.

Z merely smiled in response. Her excitement was palpable, and that made him proud.

"It's perfect! It's just like I would have imagined it. I love the white steeple rising above the landscape. It's like it is begging us to come." Cory bubbled. "Can you imagine what must have gone through their minds as they came here on Sundays. I can almost picture the wagons loaded with families coming in for church. They must have been excited that they were going to see friends and family members and spend the day worshipping God together."

As the two came out onto a flat plain, she continued, "I bet they began to see others heading toward the church from here. Can't you see them waving to one another, or maybe the kids running to each other. I bet the young girls were looking hard at the young men on horseback to see any eligible husbands."

"You can bet the young bucks were scanning the wagons for pretty girls too," he broke in to her reverie.

She stopped and smiled at him. "I'm sorry. I do go on sometimes. I really am a history geek."

"And a romantic," he added. "Don't worry. I think it's great. I've had the same thoughts myself. The people that God used to settle this land must have been amazing. We have it so easy in many ways, but without them, we wouldn't be where we are. They refused to give up and carved a life here."

"You're a history geek too," she chided, laughing.

"Guilty."

"Oh, look! It has a porch, and there's a bell in that steeple," she declared.

"Yeah, I sometimes get lost in time out here. If it starts to get dark, I will ring that bell, and Mom knows where I am and that I'm on my way home. I know that's not the original purpose of that bell, but I bet the people who heard it back then felt comfort and relief, like my mom feels when she hears it," he shared, lost in his own reverie.

Cory felt warm as she listened to him talk about this obviously special place. She could tell by his tone that this place held an important spot in his heart. Knowing that made her feel even more drawn to him. She whispered a prayer of thanks to God for this precious godly man riding beside her.

As they neared the structure, she saw that he was right. The place did need a new coat of paint, but otherwise, it looked in good shape.

"Do you want to go inside?" Z asked.

"No," Cory stated reverently.

Z was surprised. He had begun to dismount and lost sight of her prior to her response. He quickly tied off his horse and looked around at her.

She had ridden to the edge of the building and was looking around back.

"I want to go back there first," she stated.

Z smiled as he realized that she was talking about the small graveyard behind the building.

"Don't you want to go in the church first?" he asked.

"No, not yet. I want to go to the graveyard. If I am to appreciate the church like the people who built it meant for it to be appreciated, I need to get to know them." she explained. "To do that, I want a glimpse of those who wanted their memory and the memory of their loved ones forever connected to it."

She dismounted and tied her horse to the rail out front of the building. Z joined her as they walked quietly side by side around to the graveyard.

There was a well-worn path from the church to the graveyard. What once must have been a beautiful stone enclosure wound its way around the space. The stones were worn and scattered in some places. Upon closer inspection, there appeared to have been whitewash on the stones at one time. Cory commented as much as she carefully picked up a stone, examined it, and stacked it back on the wall. Both stood reverently outside the small gate for a quiet moment.

"I can only imagine that a wooden gateway must have spanned this opening. I wonder what they called this place," Cory questioned in hushed tones.

The two quietly walked through the graveyard, perusing the gravestones. Once in a while, they would read the stone aloud and ponder on the life represented there. A few times, they would call the other over to help read a particularly faded stone. They picked up falling markers and pulled up weeds, tidying the graveyard as they did so. The graves dated from the mid-1850s to the early 1900s. They ranged from newborns to a few couples in their eighties. Each one had a story, and the two living descendants speculated and honored each one.

Soon, the afternoon sun began to take its toll and beat down mercilessly. As every Texan knows, the hottest part of the day comes around three in the afternoon, and this day was no different. Despite the increasing heat, they made sure not one gravestone escaped their notice. When all were properly noted and cared for, they made their way back to the entrance.

"I wonder if there were a few graves that had wooden markers that didn't survive?" Cory asked.

"Probably," stated Z. "God, thank you for their lives too."

Cory nodded in agreement, then after a moment of silence, turned to face Z. "Okay, I'm ready now. I think I can appreciate how precious this church must have been to the people who built it. Can we go inside now?"

"Definitely." A smile spread across his face that was different. She couldn't put her finger on what the difference was. It wasn't strange or worrisome, just different—in a good way. He climbed the stairs to the porch in front of her and then turned to offer his hand.

"Miss, may I have the honor of accompanying you to church this afternoon?"

There it was. That smile again. It made her feel as if she was special, as if it was a smile for her alone.

Imagining herself as a pioneer and him as a handsome drover, she took his hand and answered in her best Texan drawl, "Why, thank you, kind sir. It would be my honor to join you this fine day."

He took her hand as she mounted the stairs, turned to unlock the door, and then placed her hand in the crook of his arm as he escorted her over the threshold and into the building.

Cory was overwhelmed. The people who had buried their loved ones out back had experienced all kinds of hardships. Disease, accidents, problem births, all the hardships of life had sought to crush them, but they had gathered here to deal with them and overcome them. Here, they sought God in good times and bad times. For baby dedications, baptisms, marriages, and funerals, here they had come together to encourage and be encouraged, to seek God and find God. In this very building, Christians from long ago had discovered the boundless mercies of a God who never changes.

She stopped Z in the doorway and squeezed his arm. He watched her and knew the emotions she was feeling. It made him glad to see her reaction. He had had the same reaction the first time he entered this place. Finally, someone else understood.

He remembered it like it was yesterday. He was probably about nineteen or twenty. He had wanted to come here, but his parents were afraid it was too dangerous. He had disobeyed them and made his way here early one morning. As he opened the door that first time, he had been overcome by the thoughts of what must have gone on in this place. He pictured the people who came here to worship God, cowboys and pioneers coming together to give thanks and lift prayers. He had convinced his parents to let him make repairs to the building. It had become his escape, his refuge. He came on weekends from college and on leave from the military. Now, he came after missions. This was the place he met with God—just as they had. This was his place. No one seemed to understand. His family respected his privacy and stayed away, but even they didn't quite understand what he felt when he was here.

Cory did. He could tell by her reaction. They stood there, taking in the scene. Rows of pews filled the bulk of the space. An aisle down the middle and each side was created by their positioning. In the front, a few pews faced the opposite way. An old piano to the side evidenced that this was obviously a choir area. Two high-backed chairs appeared to be a place for the preacher and someone else, probably a deacon or elder. To top it off, a beautifully carved pulpit in the shape of a cross stood, giving testimony that this was the place to come to hear from God, the God who had paid the highest price. Whatever burden they had, they brought it here and could lay it down.

Suddenly, Cory broke from his arm and walked to the altar and knelt.

He watched quietly as tears ran down her cheeks, and she prayed.

"They came here," she whispered, her voice touched by her tears. "Before they laid their loved ones to rest, they came here and laid down their pain...at the cross. Their pain, their fear, their failure—they brought it here." Her words hung in the air.

After a moment, Z went to the old piano. He quietly began to play "Rock of Ages." The slightly out-of-tune twang of the piano filled the sanctuary. Cory sat up on her knees.

As he finished the first stanza, he said, "They brought their praise too."

Cory looked toward him as he began to play again. She rose to her feet and began to sing:

> *Rock of Ages, cleft for me*
> *Let me hide myself in Thee*
> *Let the water and the blood*
> *From Thy wounded side which flowed*
> *Be of sin the double cure*
> *Save from wrath and make me pure.*

Seamlessly, he flowed from one old hymn to the next, and Cory followed his lead.

> *Precious Lord, take my hand; lead me on, let me stand.*
> *I am tired. I am weak. I am worn.*
> *Through the storm; through the night lead me on*
>   *to the light.*
> *Precious Lord, take my hand; lead me home.*

Shall we gather at the River, the beautiful the beautiful river
Gather with the saints at the River that flows by the throne of God.

Bringing in the sheaves, bringing in the sheaves
We shall come rejoicing bringing in the sheaves.

I am weak but Thou art strong. Jesus keep me from all wrong.
I'll be satisfied as long, as I walk, let me walk, close to Thee.
Just a closer walk with Thee; grant it Jesus is my plea.
Daily walking close to Thee. Let it be, dear Lord, let it be.

Come, Christians, join to sing. Alleluia, Amen.
Loud praise to Christ our King. Alleluia, Amen.
Let all with heart and voice, before His throne rejoice.
Praise is our gracious choice. Alleluia, Amen.

Come, thou Fount of every blessing, tune my heart to sing Thy grace;
Streams of mercy never ceasing, call for songs of loudest praise.
Teach me some melodious sonnet, sung by flaming tongues above;
Praise the mount! I'm fixed upon it, mount of Thy redeeming love.
Oh to Grace how great a debtor daily I'm constrained to be;
Let Thy grace, Lord, like a fetter bind my wand'ring heart to Thee.
Prone to wander, Lord, I feel it. Prone to leave the God I love.

*Here's my heart, Lord, take and seal it. Seal it for
Thy courts above.*

*To God be the glory, great things He hath done
So loved He the world that He gave us His Son
Who yielded His life an atonement for sin
and opened the life gate that all may go in.
Praise the Lord. Praise the Lord. Let the earth hear
His voice.
Praise the Lord. Praise the Lord. Let the people
rejoice.
Oh come to the Father through Jesus the Son
And give Him the glory great things He hath done.*

As Z worshipped at the piano, Cory moved throughout the sanctuary. She picked up an old cloth that was lying on the pulpit and began to sing and dust. A smile came to her face as she pictured a scene from a Disney movie. You know, "Whistle while you work". Just like the song said, the music took the work out of what she was doing. Cleaning the old place of dust became an act of worship.

Time passed unnoticed as the two worshipped in a building built over one hundred years ago for the purpose of worship. Time didn't matter. Only the God who was worthy of worship mattered.

That's what this place did. Priorities realigned. Fears faded. Hope burned brightly. It was the same—1850, 1950, even 2050. The reason? This was a place people turned to God. He was the focus. A heart looking for Him would find Him. Years of worship reached out to the hungry heart and drew it to the foot of the cross.

Before long, Cory finished her dusting and moved to the piano. She had found an old hymnal and placed it on the piano. Z paused in his playing to open it. The two began to play and sing some songs they didn't know. They praised and worshipped with songs new to them but not new in this place. This wasn't polished worship; it was the free worship that was sprinkled with wrong notes or wrong words and laughter. It was worship of "Oh that's good!" and "I think we messed that up." It was the genuine worship born in the moment.

Soon, Cory noticed Z straining to see the music.

"I think it's getting a little dark in here. You don't think it's going to storm again, do you?" she commented.

"I don't know. If it does, the roof will hold, and we can bring in the horses if we need to."

"Bring in the horses?" Cory questioned.

"We can't leave them out in a storm. They might get scared and hurt themselves. Besides, I bet they wouldn't be the first horses in here," he commented. "Look around on the walls and see if any of those lamps have oil in them. We can light a few."

With that, he headed outside. Cory checked the lanterns, and they did indeed have oil. She found a book of matches neatly tucked under each lantern. They were mounted on little ledges built around the room. She began to carefully light some down front. Surprisingly, they lit the space more than adequately.

"Cory!" Z called from outside. "Come here. You gotta see this."

Quickly Cory rushed outside. Z was standing down on the ground, looking back at the church. He motioned for Cory to come join him. She did.

As she turned, he pointed.

There, framed by the setting sun, stood the church. Lights twinkled from the lanterns through the old windows. Rays of light shot out from the clouds, but because of their position, they seemed to shoot out of the church itself.

Rapture rays. That's what Cory called them. When the sun shoots rays through the clouds like spotlights. Cory always imagined that is what it would look like when Christ returned to take His people home.

It was glorious. The church seemed to be wrapped by the sunlight. The church itself was rather dark with a flickering inside.

"That must be how God sees it," Cory whispered almost reverently.

"Our worship is like little flickers in the darkness, but He magnifies it and reflects His glory to the world." Z finished the thought.

They stood there and watched the sun go down.

"I guess it's not the weather," Cory stated the obvious.

"I had no idea it was getting so late. I'd better signal mom so she won't worry." Z headed back into the church to ring the bell.

Cory moved up on the porch and stood looking out. She could imagine the buggies and wagons pulling up to load up for a return trip home. She smiled with her musings and didn't even notice as Z emerged from the church and stood behind her. As she leaned on the lower railing, Z grabbed the edges of the roof above her and leaned over her shoulder.

"What do you see?" he whispered in her ear.

She smiled at the warmth of his breath on her ear. "I was imagining them getting in their wagons and buggies to head for home."

"What had they been here for? After all, it's a weekday."

"I don't know. It wasn't a funeral. I feel too full of praise," she pondered.

"Maybe it was a wedding," Z offered.

"Maybe," she answered coyly.

"I think a wedding out here would be amazing," he continued. "What do you think? Do you think you would like to have your wedding in this old place?"

Again, she was very aware of the warmth of his breath—not only his breath but his nearness. They weren't touching, but she felt the warmth of him almost wrapping around her. It took a moment to answer the question. Why was he asking? *Careful*, she warned herself.

"Oh, man, I forgot to put the fire out in the lanterns." He suddenly realized. "Stay right here. I'll go put them out and be right back. You can answer me then."

Cory stood there a bit stunned. *What should I say? What should I think?*

In the midst of her questions, something caught her eye. In the fading light, she saw movement coming out from the trees. She focused on that movement and watched as it took shape. It was a jeep. *It must be one of the boys*, she thought. *They must have gotten worried or hadn't heard the bell.*

As the jeep neared, she realized that it was not one of the boys. Behind the wheel was a beautiful blonde. The same blonde that she saw on that first day here. What was her name? Shelly. It was Shelly.

"There you are," she declared sweetly—too sweetly. It was that sugary sweet that belied the truth. "Sarah said you would be here." Taking note of Cory's position on the porch, she continued, "Oh, Ezekiel must be inside. Don't feel bad about him making you wait out here. That church is his private place. He doesn't let anyone go inside there. Not even me, and I'm his fiancé."

The word hit Cory like a gut punch. All the wind seemed to go out of her. *Fiancé?* She felt sick. A wave of nausea and confusion washed over her.

Z came back out on the porch and reacted to Shelly. "What are you doing here?"

"Your mother was getting worried," she offered.

"I rang the bell. Mom would have heard that, and she wouldn't worry," he responded. Cory was so lost in her stupor that she didn't catch the flatness in his tone. "We were headed back."

"I'll ride back with her," Cory coldly stated. "Can you please take the horse?"

It wasn't a question.

"O...kay...," Z articulated. Confused.

Cory climbed in the Jeep. Her face was pale and blank. Z was lost as he saw the look on her face.

Shelly gladly drove off and left Z to ride home with Cory's horse trailing behind him. When they arrived at the house, Cory headed straight for the bathroom without a word. She prayed that no one would see her or get in her way.

She got her prayer and made it to the bathroom without seeing anyone. They were all in the dining room.

Cory closed the lid and sat on the toilet.

She couldn't breathe.

What had just happened? The day was amazing.

What was he doing? He's engaged, and he talks to me like that?

It's happening again. He just wanted my opinion. I've let my stupid feelings get ahead of me again.

How could I have imagined that a guy like him could fall for a girl like me?

Why didn't he tell me? Why would he? He had no idea I was falling for him. He was just being nice. I'm just a friend to him!

She continued ranting at herself as she sat locked in the bathroom. When she could chastise herself no more, the tears came. She tried to stop them, but they came anyway.

Outside, Shelly had entered and let the others know she was in the bathroom. Soon, Z arrived and called for the boys to help him brush down the horses.

Cory heard the commotion and willed herself to get it together. She stood and looked in the mirror. With a prayer and a quick pep talk, she left the bathroom. She knew one thing. She had to get out of here as quickly as possible.

Slowly, she walked into the dining room. Sarah read her face immediately.

"Cory, what's wrong?" she cried, moving quickly to her side. "Are you okay?"

She couldn't pretend to be okay, so she decided to play it off. "I'm not feeling well. If we can't go home, I think I'll go lay down."

"The bridge isn't done," her father offered. "We're stuck here another night. I think we can get it fixed tomorrow though."

"Okay," she said weakly as Sarah escorted her to her room. She got the bed out and prepared it for the night. Her kindness made it even worse.

"Thank you," Cory forced out as Sarah left the room. She cried herself to sleep that night. When her father came in for bed, she pretended to be asleep and cried into her pillow quietly. By the time she fell asleep, she was thoroughly disgusted with herself and had no more tears left.

The next morning came way too soon. She made her way to the bathroom and washed her face. She realized that she had awakened before anyone this time. Quietly, she made her way outside, convinced that some fresh air would help.

Once outside, her focus moved from herself to the waking world around her. The sights and sounds of morning drew her thoughts to her Creator.

"Oh, Father, 'your mercies are new every morning.'" She quoted scripture to herself. "I need your mercies. I'm a mess. Give me strength and courage to face today."

She found a spot out behind the barn where she could watch the sunrise and the barnyard animals but still be hidden from view to anyone who wandered outside from the house. She just wasn't ready to talk to anyone.

In the stillness, God began to remind her of His love. Slowly, she began to let go of the pain or, at least, push it below the surface. She became acutely aware of what she knew for sure—God is still in control.

She realized what a gift the Christian family was to her father, and to her. They had become, and would remain, good friends. For her father's sake, she needed to deal with her feelings for Z. He was a good friend. She just needed to be better at guarding her heart.

Soon, she realized that she was probably missed. It was almost noon when she headed back to the house. She was met on the porch by Abigail.

"There you are. Are you feeling better this morning?" she asked with genuine concern.

"I'll be okay. I just awoke and needed some fresh air," Cory replied.

"Mom said I should let you have some space. She always seems to have a feel for these things," Abigail commented. "You know, if you need someone to talk to, you can talk to me or Mom. We're really good listeners."

Cory smiled as she looked at the kind, concerned woman in front of her. "Thank you, Abigail. I want you to know that I believe that, and if I need to talk, I will definitely come to you. I hope we can become really good friends."

Abigail reached out and hugged Cory. "I'd like that very much," she said.

The two women walked inside together, Abigail quietly respecting Cory's need for space. When they reached the kitchen, Sarah was busily finalizing lunch preparations.

"There you are," she said cheerfully. "I hope you feel like lunch. We're gonna eat in here today before you and your dad head home. They boys have the bridge up and ready to go. They'll be here soon."

Cory swallowed hard. Sarah didn't miss it.

"You do feel like eating, don't you?" she rushed to Cory's side, concerned.

"I'm okay," Cory covered. Her heart began to warm with the genuine concern she felt from both these wonderful women. She realized that they truly could be wonderful friends. "I'd just like a glass of water to sip."

Sarah got her some water, and Cory sat at the counter.

There was a commotion in the yard out front, and soon, the screen door was slamming, and the boys rumbled through the living room and into the kitchen. They said their hellos and washed up. Jim and Bob were next in to wash up. Soon, Ezekiel came in as well. When they were all washed up, the boys and older men came in and took their place around the table.

Cory remained at the counter.

When Ezekiel entered, he came over to Cory and gently placed his hand on her shoulder. "Are you okay?" he asked quietly.

Cory could hear the genuine concern through her hurt and prayed for the strength to respond. *He's clueless,* she thought. *He has no idea how I feel.* In a way that helped. She just couldn't imagine that he was such a cad as to knowingly lead her on while being engaged. It went against everything she knew about him.

"I'll be all right. I just need some rest. It's been an eventful few days." She smiled weakly in his direction but couldn't meet his eyes.

He moved to the table, and they shared a pleasant lunch. Cory found herself watching the developing friendship between her father and this family. She had to find a way to deal with this feeling she had inside.

It wasn't long before lunch was over, and feeling her need to get home, her father rose and offered his goodbyes and promises to stay in touch. With little fanfare, they soon were in her truck and headed for home.

Cory was quiet. Her father sensed something was really wrong, but knowing his daughter, he gave her space to think things through. When they got home, he simply said, "Let me know if you need anything. I'm here."

Cory hadn't taken a vacation this summer, so now seemed the perfect time. She chose to spend some time with her sister. This was just far enough away that she could disconnect, but no so far that she had to make plans or spend a lot of money. Her sister was always glad for the company, and the time was extremely therapeutic.

Cory hadn't told her sister about Z. How thankful she was of that fact. There was no explaining to do, and she could throw herself into time with her two nephews. They were busy enough that she found herself pleasantly diverted.

Through it all, God continued to teach Cory to trust. She knew He had a plan. She also knew she had to trust that plan. She didn't need to understand it; she just needed to trust. These days with her sister gave her a chance to re-anchor herself.

Before long, she headed home and back to her routine. She returned to church, and Z wasn't there. Her father informed her that he had been called out on duty again. While Cory prayed for his safety, she was also grateful she didn't have to face him just yet.

She dove into the new school year and immersed herself in schoolwork. The longer he was gone, the more she prayed for his return. She found she missed his friendship. That was where she found a place to stand. They were to be friends. She prayed God would steel her heart and allow their friendship to become strong. She determined to tightly hold the reigns of her heart.

It happened in December. School was out for the holidays. The phone rang.

It was Sarah. Cory could hear the worry in her voice. "Cory? I hate to ask this, but we need you." The silence hung in the air.

"What's wrong? What do you need?" Cory asked.

"He's not okay," she stated flatly. "He came home this time and won't talk to anyone. He's holed up in the church. I'm worried. I don't know what happened that day before you left, but Ezekiel told me you spent the day in the church with him. He lets no one in there, but he let you. Could you come talk to him? I'm scared. He's strong, but I've heard stories of soldiers doing terrible things—" She broke into tears.

Cory's heart froze. "Do you really think he's in trouble?" she asked.

"I do." She spoke through her emotion.

All apprehension was gone. He needed her. They needed her. "I'll be there as soon as I can."

Quickly, she related to her father the situation.

"Go," he said, "and I'll be praying for you."

She got in her truck and left immediately. While driving, the radio played in the background. A song by the J.J. Weeks band came over the airwaves. "Let them see You, in me. Let them hear you when I speak. Let them see You when I sing. Let them see You; let them see You in me." *Oh, God, that's the prayer of my heart. Do it now as never before*, she prayed.

Cory didn't even stop at the house. She drove straight to the church. As she got out of her truck, she stopped.

"Oh God, perhaps you have put me here 'for such a time as this.' Guide my thoughts and words. Use me to help him."

She walked up the steps and to the door. Quietly, she strained to hear any sound or evidence that he was inside.

Nothing.

"Z," she said into the door. "Are you in there?"

Nothing.

"Z," she said louder. "Are you here?"

She waited. Nothing. *What should I do?* she asked God.

Suddenly a tune entered her thoughts. She moved to the rail and began to sing.

> *I know not why God's wondrous grace to me He*
> *hath made known,*
> *Nor why unworthy, Christ in love, redeemed me for*
> *His own.*
> *But I know Whom I have believed and am per-*
> *suaded that He is able*
> *To keep that which I've committed unto Him*
> *against that day.*
>
> *I know not how this saving faith to me He did*
> *impart,*
> *Nor how believing in His Word wrought peace*
> *within my heart.*
> *But I know Whom I have believed and am per-*
> *suaded that He is able*
> *To keep that which I've committed unto Him*
> *against that day.*
>
> *I know not how the Spirit moves, convincing men*
> *of sin.*

Quietly, the door opened behind Cory, and a strong male voice joined in song

> *Revealing Jesus thro' the Word, creating faith in Him.*
> *But I know Whom I have believed, and am per-*
> *suaded that He is able*
> *To keep that which I've committed unto Him*
> *against that day.*

Cory continued staring out, but her voice trailed off. The male voice continued.

> *I know not when my Lord may come, at night or*
> *noon-day fair*
> *Nor if I'll walk the vale with Him, or meet Him in*
> *the air.*
> *But I know Whom I have believed and am per-*
> *suaded that He is able*
> *To keep that which I've committed unto Him*
> *against that day.*

Slowly, she turned toward the door. It was only slightly open. "You can come in," the voice offered.

Quietly, she pushed open the door and walked into the dark room. Unlike her first time in this room, she was not overwhelmed with a heart to worship. This time, her eyes searched the darkness for a hurting soul.

He sat on the back pew. His head was bowed and, for the first time since she'd known him, shoulders slumped. He looked small and lonely and hurt. Despite her best efforts to control her heart, it reached out for him.

She knew better than to say anything. She moved to the pew and quietly sat next to him.

In silence, they sat for a long time.

He broke the silence. "I know Whom I have believed and am persuaded that He is able to keep that which I've committed unto Him against that day." He requoted the scripture from the song. "I do believe, but I don't understand." The pain in his voice was raw and hung in the air.

Again, she remained quiet. How could she say anything? She had no idea what he had gone through or what he was feeling. She hoped her presence was enough.

When he looked her way, those eyes looked tired and sad...oh, so sad.

Only this morning, she had wondered how she could ever look in those eyes again without letting him see her hurt. Now, all she cared about was the pain she saw in those eyes. Her own hurt was nowhere to be found. When he looked into her eyes, he saw only the reflection of His Savior.

"You said once you would listen if I needed you to. Did you mean it?" He broke the silence.

Without a word, she held his gaze and nodded.

"I couldn't stop it." The pain from his eyes twisted his face. It seemed the flood of thoughts contorted his entire body. Slowly he began to pour out his heart.

She listened and shared in his pain. She sat quiet when he sat quiet. She cried when he cried. Most of all, she ached as he ached.

He spoke until he could no longer speak. She opened her hand and lay it on the pew between them. He looked down and smiled, remembering the night she poured her heart out to him. He dropped his hand into hers. She tightly grasped his hand.

He looked up at her again. "Can I ask you something?"

Again, she nodded without a word.

"Would you…" he paused as if not sure.

She knew instinctively what he needed. Without hesitation, she moved closer to him and wrapped her arms around him.

As he felt her arms around him, all of his defenses broke down. The tears came.

It wasn't a passionate embrace. He felt safe and let himself be vulnerable. He cried and cried as she quietly held him. It seemed all the pain he held inside drained out of him. Cory closed her eyes and prayed for God to bring him comfort. She knew that only God could heal the wounds he had experienced. God had chosen him to walk this path, and she knew He would be strong in Z's weakness. Before long, her tears intermingled with his as they fell to the floor of the old church. There they sat for God only knows how long. Once again, time had come to a standstill.

When both had seemingly cried all the tears possible, and the quaking in his body ceased, Cory opened her eyes. Her gaze fell on the cross-shaped pulpit.

The sun was going down, and a ray of light shown through the window and fell directly on the cross.

"Z," Cory whispered into his ear. "Look"

He lifted his head and followed her gaze. As he saw what she saw, he slowly stood to his feet.

Cory watched as he stood staring for a moment and then moved to the cross.

Another solitary tear slipped down his cheek. He dropped to his knees. After a moment, he broke the silence.

"He understands," Z said. "Remember after we sang that old hymn, I said I believed, but I didn't understand? Well"—he pointed to the cross—"He's telling me He understands."

As he looked at her, she saw the light come back into his eyes. Her heart filled with warmth. He looked back to the cross.

As he did, she found herself praying again for this brave man who carried such a heavy load.

The two stayed as they were until the ray of light slowly moved with the setting sun, out of sight. In the last vestiges of light, Cory moved to his side and placed her hand on his shoulder.

He reached up and touched her hand. The gesture was a kind of unspoken "thank you."

Quietly, he stood and moved to the piano. As the room grew dark, he began to play from memory. The soft strains of a song filled the room.

Cory listened in the dark for a moment and then felt her way to the wall. She felt along the wall until her hand fell on what she was looking for. In only a moment, she grabbed the lantern and matches and lit the wick.

As the lamp sprang to life, she moved to the piano, and the two sang the beloved Gaither chorus together.

> *Because He lives, I can face tomorrow.*
> *Because He lives all fear is gone.*
> *Because I know, I know, He holds the future,*
> *And life is worth the living just because He lives.*

As the last notes of the piano floated into the distance, Z rose from the piano and took the lantern from her hand. Grasping her hand in his other hand, he led her to the door of the church. He pushed it open and blew out the lantern. Gently, he set the lantern on a back pew, then turned to Cory.

"Could I get a lift back to the house?" he asked meekly.

"I think that could be arranged, but I'd feel better if you'd drive. I don't think I could find my way in the dark." she confessed.

"Gladly," he responded.

The two climbed in the truck. Suddenly, Z stopped. "Wait one minute," he said and left the truck.

Cory watched as he bounded up the steps. She couldn't see what he was doing no matter how hard she strained. It was late and dark.

Through the darkness and the sounds of nature, Cory heard the loud peal of the steeple bell. It rang boldly, piercing the night.

Soon, she picked up movement, and it wasn't long before he was back in the truck. As he put the key in the ignition, he smiled her way. "I thought I'd better send my mother a message. I know she's worried."

Cory smiled back. As she did, she realized how she had missed that smile and those eyes.

It wasn't long before the main house came into view. Standing on the lighted porch was Sarah. She stood with her hand over her mouth, watching the truck with anticipation. When Z emerged, she began to cry. She threw her arms open, and he skipped the bottom stair as he flung himself into her arms.

"It's okay, Mom." Cory could hear him comfort her. "I'm okay."

As they embraced, Jim came out on the porch. With no less emotion, Z moved from his mother to his father. The two men embraced.

As they did so, Sarah moved to the truck. She grabbed Cory and held her tight.

"Thank you sooooo much," she said through her tears.

Cory hugged her back, then attempted to move to the driver's side of the truck. She felt the desire to leave these sweet people to love on one another.

Z and Jim had come down off the porch.

"Where do you think you are going, young lady?" Jim scolded.

"I wanted to leave you to your privacy. I should be getting home. Dad will be worried," she explained.

"He's not worried. I just got off the phone with him. I called him when we heard the church bell," Jim informed her. "Now, you come on inside with us."

"How could I refuse?" she acquiesced.

The four of them moved up on the porch and then inside. They sat in the living room and talked. Before they knew it, it was late.

Cory rose, "I'd better be getting home. It's really late, and I have a bit of a drive."

"Actually," Jim inserted, "I told your dad I wouldn't let you drive home late. I told him I'd get you to stay here. You can stay in Abigail's old room."

Though surprised that her father and Jim had made plans for her, she couldn't be mad as she looked at Jim's kind face. It was nice to know they were looking out for her. She really didn't want to drive home after such a draining evening.

"Okay. How could I say no?" She smiled at the older gentleman.

"Before we go to bed, could we pray together?" Jim requested.

The quartet joined hands, bowed their heads, and Jim led them in a prayer together. He eloquently led them to the throne of grace, and together, they praised God and laid their requests at His feet and gave thanks. At the end, they said "Amen" in unison and said their good nights before heading off to bed.

The next morning, Cory awoke feeling rested. It was the middle of the morning, and she felt bad sleeping in but knew she needed it. Sometimes, being emotionally exhausted can only be remedied by sleep.

When she emerged from her room, she found Sarah sitting in the kitchen, with her Bible open on the counter in front of her.

"Good morning," Cory greeted her.

"Well, good morning," she cheerfully responded. "Would you like some breakfast?"

"No, thank you. I should be getting home," Cory said

"Listen, Ezekiel and Jim are down working in the barn. They should be finished soon, and Ezekiel asked me to ask you to wait for him. I think he wanted to say goodbye," Sarah said in an almost pleading tone.

Cory smiled. "Well—"

Cutting her off before she could say no, Sarah interjected, "Hey, I was working on your Christmas gift and was wondering if I could get you to try it on for me. It will kinda spoil the surprise, but I'd rather do that and have it fit than surprise you with something you can't wear."

"You're making something for me?" Cory questioned with genuine surprise. "You don't have to get me a Christmas present."

"Maybe not, but I want to," Sarah said with conviction. "Besides, I miss getting to make clothes for a girl. I used to love to make pretty things for Abigail."

The two ladies laughed, and Cory consented. The result was an hour or so of pampering for Cory. Sarah busied herself with sewing, hair, and makeup. She was in hog heaven. She not only liked doing these things, she was good at it. She seemed to have an eye for what would look good.

Just as Sarah was putting the finishing touches on her project, the two women heard the screen door open and slam shut. There were voices that could be made out if you strained to listen—and they did.

"I can't believe you." It was Shelly. "What do you see in her? She's not very pretty, and she's kinda—"

"Shut up!" That was Z, and he was angry.

Sarah and Cory looked at one another. The look in Sarah's eye said she had heard that tone before, and it was not good. She quickly headed to intervene. Cory stayed where she was.

"Hello!" Sarah called as if unaware of the fight that was happening in the living room.

Shelly's demeanor changed. That sugary sweet tone replaced the accusatory one. "Well, hello, Mrs. Christian."

Sarah acknowledged her with a nod, then addressed Z. "Ezekiel, I convinced Cory to stay."

Those words made Cory freeze. She didn't want to be in the middle of a fight between the couple. She quietly prayed that Sarah would change the subject.

She didn't.

"Cory," she called. "Come out here and see what Ezekiel thinks of my Christmas present."

"Christmas?" Shelly questioned. "It's not Christmas yet."

"I know," Sarah responded. "But I needed to make sure it fits, and since I've got her here, I decided to put on the finishing touches. Now that you're here, Ezekiel, you can be honest about how it looks."

"She's still here?" he said, a smile spreading across his face, a fact which was not lost on Shelly. "I'd be glad to tell you what I think. I'm sure it looks great."

"Cory?" Sarah beckoned again.

She had frozen when Sarah brought her into the conversation. She wanted to disappear and let the engaged couple deal with the situation, but she had gotten the distinct impression that, though Sarah was kind and gentle, she had the same stubborn streak as Z. It was obvious that she was intentionally inserting Cory. She had kept her here to talk with Z, and she was making sure he knew of her presence.

She looked at the window in the room and briefly pondered how easy it would be to climb out it and get to her truck. A smile curled her lips as she thought how silly she was being. She quietly argued with herself about whether or not she should go into that living room. It seemed like forever, but it was only a moment before she knew what she had to do.

Giving in to her better angels, Cory came into the living room. As she did so, the surprise on Shelly's face was priceless. Cory couldn't help but smile as she saw the look. Sheepishly, she then looked toward Z.

"Wow!" he said. "You look amazing."

Sarah was indeed a good seamstress. Cory hadn't had a custom-made outfit since she was young. The dress felt good, and it made her look good. Sarah's beautician skills were excellent as well, and when she saw Z's face, she felt beautiful.

Cory shyly smiled at Z and mouthed "thank you" to Sarah who beamed with pride.

Sarah boldly took control of the awkward situation as only a mother can do. "All right, we can't stand around here all day. Ezekiel, please go get your father from the barn for lunch. Shelly, if you are staying for lunch, go clean up. Cory, come help me in the kitchen."

Instinctively, each sprang to action just as Sarah commanded. Before long, the kitchen was a hub of activity as the table was set and lunch was made and placed on the table. Shelly joined Cory and Sarah in the kitchen after she cleaned up, and the three had everything ready when the men came to the table.

The small group chatted, and before long, Sarah rose from the table. "Shelly, help me clean up this mess. Cory, go change your clothes, so I can finish it up and wrap it for Christmas."

Again, each obediently carried out Sarah's instructions.

Cory headed back to the bedroom and carefully changed out of the beautiful dress. She couldn't stop the smile that spread across her face as she thought of the time and love that Sarah had put into that dress. She hadn't had someone take that much time for her in a long time. It didn't hurt that it was the perfect style and made her feel great.

A small tablet on the table next to the sewing machine caught her eye. Picking it up and finding a pencil, she wrote a quick thank you note and left it for Sarah to find. She'd forgotten how much she missed the pampering that only a mother could give. Despite the situation with Ezekiel and Shelly, Cory realized that God had gifted her with this whole family. She had let her feelings blind her to the precious friends God had given her and her father.

Looking around, she realized that, with that admission, God had given her the strength to deal with her feelings for Ezekiel. She looked in the mirror.

"Wow! What a difference hair and makeup can make in how you feel. I look new, and I feel new. Thanks, God!" With that, she walked out of the room.

Shelly and Sarah were still busy in the kitchen. Cory really didn't want to be in there with Shelly. That was still a sore spot. She decided to go out on the porch and just soak in the beauty that God had put all around her.

The cool breeze that met her as she opened the door and walked out on the porch was refreshing. It was a typical cool Texas December. The snow, or ice, in Texas didn't come—if it came at all—until February, but it did cool off. She walked to the rail on the porch and took a deep breath of the fresh, cool air.

In her focus on the fresh air, she hadn't seen that Z was seated in a rocking chair at the edge of the porch.

He smiled as he watched her breathe in deeply and close her eyes. He wondered what she was thinking but knew she was probably talking to God. The slight upturn on her lips made him think she was thanking him.

He took advantage of the moment to drink in the sight of her. His mother had indeed done her magic with hair and makeup, but that's not what he saw. His mind replayed all the ways God had used this precious woman to minister to him. He couldn't help but think back to their quiet moments in the church. She had no idea all that he was dealing with, but she was there. She listened without trying to "fix" things. She had taken in all the things he shared with her and not flinched.

This was the most godly woman he had ever met. This was the most beautiful woman he had ever met. She had no idea all that he saw in her, and that was another part of her beauty. He quietly thanked God for this precious woman.

As he did so, he noticed something on the rafter above Cory's head. Z squinted to see what it was. He looked up at the rafter above himself and saw the same thing. Realizing what his mother had placed all around the porch along with her Christmas decorations, he smiled.

With intent in his steps, he moved toward Cory.

"Well, hello there," he said as he moved to her side.

Opening her eyes with a start, Cory turned to see Z standing right next to her.

"Hello," she said

"Sorry, I didn't mean to startle you. I just noticed you enjoying a Texas December and thought I'd join you," he spoke with a smile.

She smiled and looked to the floor.

Z took the move as shyness and stepped closer, putting his arms around her. "I wanted to thank you for last night," he shared softly.

She stiffened a bit at his embrace, but with his words, she looked up into his eyes and softened.

"I was in a really dark place, and you were there for me."

Uncomfortable with his embrace—or perhaps, uncomfortable that she was so comfortable with his embrace—she tried to step back away from him. *I can't let my feelings take over. He only thinks of me as a friend*, she warned herself.

"That's what friends are for," she said, trying to be light and whimsical.

Feeling her pulling away, he replied, "Wait a minute. You wouldn't want to destroy centuries of Christmas tradition, would you?" He pulled her close and, with his head, nodded to the mistletoe hanging above them.

As Cory looked up to see the Christmas fungus, she felt a cold wash over her.

He's my friend, tell him, she thought.

He had noticed the chill, and it confused him. "If the thought of kissing me is that awful..." he offered playfully—sort of.

"No, it's not that," she responded, quickly thinking, *just the opposite*. "It's just that, well, promise you won't laugh at me."

He held her in his arms and promised, "I would never laugh at you—with you, but not at you. What is it?"

"Well, remember I told you when we first met that I hadn't been on any dates."

He nodded.

"That was true. Because of that, I never kissed anyone. Oh, my parents, on the cheek, or my nephews, on the head, but not kissed. I'm a typical girl, and that bothered me for a long time. I wanted to know what it was like and felt I was a freak. It wasn't until I was older that I realized that God knew my heart much better than I knew my heart. He was, in a way, protecting me. I realized that, for me, a kiss wasn't just something you do. It had meaning. It wasn't, 'I had a nice time' or 'Thank you' or 'I'm sorry' or 'I hope you feel better' or 'I wonder what it's like.' I realized that when I kiss someone, it means one thing. 'I love you.' Because of that, when I am comfortable enough to kiss someone on the lips, it will be because I am saying, 'I love you,' and it won't matter if that person loves me or not. It just means that I love them, and they have my heart no matter what. I won't be able to take it back because I believe the Bible when it says 'love never fails.' I can't just kiss you because of some tradition. Does that make sense?" she finished quietly.

He held her for a moment. A warmth filled his heart as he looked at this incredibly unique woman. He nodded his understanding, then motioned for her to sit with him on the swing.

"Maybe I'm just kidding myself. Maybe it's just a way for me to deal with being too fat and not pretty enough for a boyfriend. Everybody always says I look at the world differently," she muttered under her breath as she flopped onto the swing.

"What?" Z stopped before sitting and squared around to look at her.

"Did I say that out loud?" she looked up in horror.

"Yes, you did. And you just listen to me." He began towering over her. "You DO look at the world differently. You see it as God does. You see it the way I always want to see it. I don't ever want you to listen to whatever demonic voice put that last thought in your head!"

He sat next to her on the swing, and his voice softened. "Ever since I met you, the most amazing thing about you was that you saw the world differently. I have always been accused of that, and now, I met someone who seemed to be right there with me. I realized that's because of our love for God. He has changed the way we see things, and when we listen to Him, this world is an amazing place. But I'll be honest, I have to fight thoughts of inadequacy too.

"Remember when Samuel was looking to anoint a new king? God said no to all the tall, strong men paraded before him. When he finally brought out a scrawny, young redhead, God said, 'That's him.' Samuel didn't understand. He didn't look like a king. God informed him that 'God sees not as man sees. For man looks at the outward appearance. God looks at the heart.'

"That's what I see when I look at you. I see a beautiful heart. That's what the people that should matter to you see as well. That's what causes you to see the true beauty that is hidden in a kiss. Others may not see that, but you do. If Satan can get you to lose focus, he'll try to twist what you see, to make you see what the lost world sees. The problem with that is the world is never satisfied. No one looks good enough. Keep listening to what God says. See the world as He does. Help others see it too."

"I thought you said you weren't a preacher like your father," she said, lightening the mood. "That's a pretty good sermon if you ask me."

He returned her smile and asked, "Did it work?"

"I think I get the message. I just can't believe we see the world so differently," she commented as they slowly swayed in the swing.

"Oh yeah?" he challenged. "Watch this." He looked around, then seeing what he was looking for, pointed to the corral. "Look over there and tell me what you see. Describe it for me."

She followed his outstretched arm, and there, slowly meandering from the barn out toward a water trough, under a stand of trees, was a horse.

"Okay." She played along. "I see a beautiful creature with a golden-brown coat and powerful body. It majestically shakes the black strands of its mane to shoo away flies like a supermodel on a Paris runway." She paused to giggle. "I have to admit, there's something about the smell of a sweaty horse and hot leather. I think it's amazing. I don't see how you could look at that magnificent creature and believe it was a random accident of nature. I see a perfect example of the creativity of God. How wonderful is God to give us the ability to have a relationship with horses!"

He laughed at the melodramatic response and then nodded in agreement to her final comments. "I agree. I love rubbing down the horses after a long day. It just makes me thank God for them. I can't imagine life without horses. But not everyone sees things like we do."

He leaned back in the swing and shouted, "Hey, Shelly! Can you come here a minute please?"

"Watch this," he whispered.

Shelly came from the kitchen out onto the porch. "Yes, Ezekiel?" she began in that sugary tone and then changed when she saw the two on the swing.

"What do you need?" she finished flatly.

"Look over there and tell me what you see," he said, pointing to the same horse.

"What?" she said, straining to see what he was pointing at. "You mean that nasty horse over there? You know I can't stand those smelly things. I don't even know why they exist. We have cars now. What a useless waste."

With that, she exhaled in disgust and put her hands on her hips.

Both Ezekiel and Cory struggled to suppress grins. He had made his point. She obviously did not see the world as they did.

Cory couldn't help but wonder in her spirit, *Then why in the world did he ask her to marry him?*

In the midst of her query and Shelly's disgust came the shrill ring of a phone. A frown crossed Z's brow. It was his phone. He answered it and walked down from the porch, gesturing his apology.

It was obvious to the women that the call was important. About that time, Sarah joined them outside.

Ezekiel sat on the tailgate of his truck as he spoke into the phone. There were a lot of "Yes, Sir," and Cory knew it was the military. Cory's heart cried "not now." She knew God was in control, but after the last evening, she wasn't sure he was ready for another mission.

He hung up the phone, stating what they all already knew. "I have to go—again."

Cory expected to hear the flat tone. She didn't.

Instead, Shelly exploded with drama. "Nooooo," she cried loudly. "You can't leave us. We need you. How could you do this to us? You can't imagine the worry we go through!"

As Shelly whined and begged, anger began to build inside Cory. She scolded herself. She had no business getting in the middle of their argument. After all, they were engaged. They needed to learn to work out their differences. She willed herself to stay out of it.

"What would we do if something happened to you? Think about us for a change!" Shelly continued to whine.

Finally, Cory had had enough. He had experienced a walk way too close to the edge for her last night, and he didn't need Shelly giving him a shove over that edge now.

"Shut up!" Cory exploded at Shelly. "How dare you! How dare you react like that! Can't you think about anyone but yourself? Don't you get it? This isn't about you! If you cared at all about him, you'd stop talking right now."

Cory physically placed herself in the line of sight so Z couldn't see Shelly. She made sure he was looking directly at her.

"Now, you listen to me. Don't you worry a minute about us. We will be just fine. You go do what God wants—needs you to do. God will take care of us, and He will take care of you." She paused, searching for words.

She wanted to somehow fill him with all of the strength she could muster. As she searched for what to say or do, she realized a truth.

She loved him.

She knew it was true.

Even if he never loved her, she knew she loved him.

In that split moment, she didn't care about her own feelings. She just wanted him to know he wasn't alone.

"You can go do this. God is sending you, and I want you to take my strength with you." She paused again. "I wish I knew how to give you my strength," she said as she stood before him peering into his eyes.

Then it hit her. She knew.

Without hesitation, she took a step toward him and kissed him. She felt no fear, no inhibitions. She just willed all of her strength to him.

He responded.

As their lips parted, she whispered, "Take my strength with you. No matter what, I will be praying for you, and I KNOW God will take care of all of us."

She turned to walk away. As she did, she saw Shelly standing there, stunned.

"I'm sorry for yelling at you, but I can't let you do that to him. If you truly love him and are to be married, you better figure it out." With that, she climbed behind the wheel of her truck and started the engine.

Z stood there, stunned. The import of that kiss was not lost on him. He had dreamed of kissing her, and it was everything he dreamed of, but what had happened next caught him off guard.

What had she said to Shelly?

She thought he was gonna marry Shelly?

He looked over at Shelly. "What have you done? What did you tell her?" he spat in anger.

She bowed her head in shame and walked away.

He ran toward the bridge.

Cory thought she should be crying, but no tears came. She loved him, and she had intervened, but she had let him go. It was gonna be okay. God had used her, and that felt right. God had allowed her to know what love felt like, even if He also taught her the feeling of loss.

"What?" she exclaimed.

Z stood blocking the bridge.

She slammed on the brakes.

He didn't move.

She rolled down the window. "What are you doing?" She shouted out the window.

He said nothing and didn't move.

She opened the door and got out of the truck.

This time, he came over to her and took her by the hand. He led her to the creek side.

There, hanging from a tree very near the bank, was a rope.

He wrapped his arm around her and looked deeply in her eyes. "Do you trust me?"

He read the question in her eyes and repeated himself. "Do you trust me?"

"Yes," she whispered.

"Then hold on," he said as he lifted her off her feet, grabbed the rope, and swung across the creek.

When they landed on the other side, he set her down but didn't remove his arms or let her move hers.

"What was that for?" Cory asked, breathless and confused.

"Now, you listen to me," he said sternly. "You not only say you trust me, but you just proved it, so I want you to hear what I have to say. I have no idea what Shelly led you to believe. I know it happened after our time in the church. I couldn't understand what happened to you on the ride home. I could tell by your face something was terribly wrong. Now I know. Whatever she said, she lied."

He paused and waited.

"She told me she was your fiancé." Cory could barely say the words.

"She is not now, nor has she ever been, nor will she ever be my fiancé. I have only ever loved one woman." He paused for affect. "You."

At that moment, a car drove up. James and John jumped out.

"Hey, you guys!" they shouted greetings.

Z gently traced the edge of her cheek with his finger before letting her go and walking over to the boys.

"Okay, I'm gonna take your car. I'll get it back to you, and you can use my truck in the meantime. Now, remember what I asked you to do for me?"

The two boys seemed to grin all over with excitement.

"Well, when I'm gone, you do it all right?"

They both tackled him and responded with "you bet" and "we got this." The three hugged and parted.

Z walked around to the driver's side of the car, then looked back at Cory standing near the creek.

"Hey, wait a minute," she yelled at him. "How am I supposed to get back over there?"

With a twinkle in his eye, he yelled back, "How's your Tarzan yell?"

They both laughed, and she replied, "I think I'll use the bridge."

With that, he waved and drove away. Cory and the boys walked back across the bridge.

Cory had been stunned with the events of that day. When she and the boys got back to the house, only Sarah was still there. She had that look of knowing that only a mother can have. She must have also known that Cory's head was spinning, so she said nothing more than "Is everyone okay?"

The boys responded with an explanation of the events on the other side of the creek. Cory was really glad they were here to save her from having to talk. She wasn't sure she could right now. As the boys talked, they all walked back to the porch.

The boys and Sarah went up on the porch. Cory stopped.

"I think I'll head home now," she managed to get out.

"Wait," said James. "Before you go, we need you to do something for us."

"Yeah," finished John. "We need you to come back here tomorrow about two o'clock. Uncle Z made us promise to give you something."

"He said it had to be at two o'clock and right here. Will you come?" James pleaded.

Cory was just a bit flustered. She looked at the two young men and thought, *How can I say no to those precious faces?*

"Okay." she gave in. "I'll be here tomorrow at two."

With an appropriate show of glee, the boys said their goodbyes, and Cory headed home.

Just as promised, Cory drove across the bridge at exactly 2:00 pm. She had spent the whole evening recounting the events of the day to her father and best friend. Then she prayed the night away, for Ezekiel, for herself, for them both. She even prayed with a bit of apprehension for today. All the speculation seemed to come to a head as she emerged in front of the house.

There on the porch was the whole family. Sarah and Jim sat in the swing. Abigail was perched on the railing drinking a glass of tea, and the boys were seated on the steps.

Cory parked the truck and joined them on the porch.

"Right on time," James said, bounding over to her and giving her a hug.

"I'm so excited!" John added as he hugged her too.

"Well, I don't know what you guys have up your sleeve, but how could I resist these two handsome fellows," Cory said, standing between them.

"All right." James took the lead. "Uncle Z gave us specific directions."

"He said to give you this note at as close to 2:00 pm as possible," finished John.

Cory took the letter and began to read on the outside flap of the folded note

> I wanted to be with you as you did this, but if you are reading this note from the boys, that means I must be deployed. Since that is the case, you must know that the adventure you are about to go on is important to me. I want you to finish reading this letter, then take everyone with you as you do what it says. I don't want to say much more except, I love you, and we'll talk more when I get home.

Smiling with warmth as she read that line, she unfolded the paper. The handwriting changed. He obviously wrote the first part at a different time than when he wrote the rest of this. The writing was print now. The previous had been cursive.

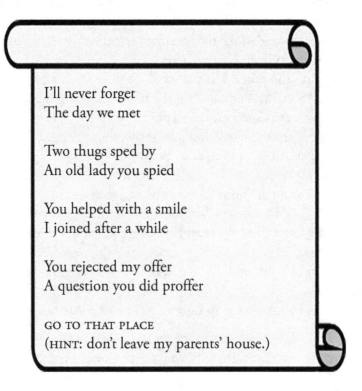

I'll never forget
The day we met

Two thugs sped by
An old lady you spied

You helped with a smile
I joined after a while

You rejected my offer
A question you did proffer

GO TO THAT PLACE
(HINT: don't leave my parents' house.)

Cory looked up at the family now standing in front of her.

"What is it?" Abigail asked. "Can you tell us what it says?"

"It's a scavenger hunt, Mom," James answered. "We have to use this as a clue to find the next one."

"I think he's right," Cory confirmed. She read the poem out loud.

"It's a little simple, but I had no idea Ezekiel could write poetry," Abigail commented.

"Whatever," Sarah brushed the sibling rivalry aside. "What does it mean, Cory?"

Cory explained the events of their first meeting in the parking lot of Kroger. Sarah and Abigail responded with the appropriate oohs and aahhs.

"Okay, you hopelessly romantic women. Where does he want us to go?" Jim scolded, getting them back on task.

"Yeah, we don't have any gas pumps on the ranch," James pointed out.

"No," Cory said thoughtfully. "But my truck is here."

As realization flooded her thoughts, she rushed to her truck. "We stood back here at the gas tank."

Quickly, Cory flipped open the cover on the side of the truck. There, duct taped to the door, was another note. She quickly opened it and read it aloud.

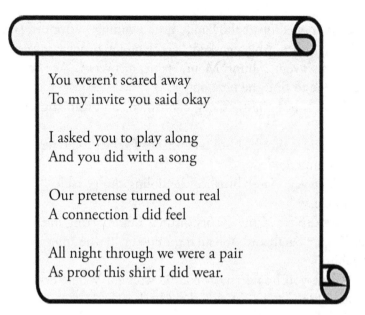

You weren't scared away
To my invite you said okay

I asked you to play along
And you did with a song

Our pretense turned out real
A connection I did feel

All night through we were a pair
As proof this shirt I did wear.

"Where are we supposed to go?" John asked.

"Well, he seems to be referring to the shirts we wore," Cory said. "Does he have any clothes at the house?"

Sarah perked up. "Of course, he does. He keeps an apartment near the seminary, but he still pretty much lives here. Let's check his room."

The group moved inside. Sarah thumbed through the drawers, and Abigail checked the closet. Despite a few comments on his clothing choices from Abigail, it was Sarah who found the shirt.

"This must be it." She held up the purple shirt with "STUPID" written across the front.

"Okay," said Jim. "What's the story of this awful shirt?"

Again, Cory shared the story of their night at the seminary party. Obviously, Z had told them about Amber. They all had a few comments about her attempts to insert herself at functions they had attended at the seminary. They commented too on the Geoffreys.

As soon as she had picked up the shirt, Sarah had felt the note concealed inside, but she kept it from view until Cory had told the entire story. She was loving this wonderful show-and-tell. She made a note to thank her son for being so creative.

118

"Here's the next clue." Sarah handed Cory the note.

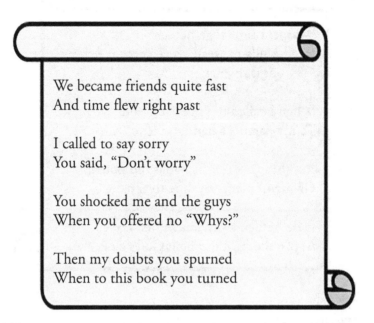

We became friends quite fast
And time flew right past

I called to say sorry
You said, "Don't worry"

You shocked me and the guys
When you offered no "Whys?"

Then my doubts you spurned
When to this book you turned

"I know what he's talking about." Sarah broke in. "He told me how you helped him see how God could and did call men to be warriors."

"Then he must have a Bible around here somewhere," Abigail added.

John found it. "Here it is, but I want to hear the story first."

Cory obliged and told them the story.

"So we need to turn to the book of Joshua, don't you think?" John responded as he handed the Bible to Cory.

"You're right!" she smiled as a note appeared in the open Bible.

We spent time together
In all kinds of weather. (I know it's cheesy,
  but it rhymes. ☺)

When I called this special friend
To my parents a hand did lend

But the creek o'er its banks did pour
Giving us plenty of time to explore

Here hidden away this flower alone
At just the right moment God's glory shone.

"It's time to take a trip," Cory said.

"We'll get the jeep," James offered in excitement. Jim nodded, and the boys ran toward the barn.

"I'll let them drive it over here, but then I'll take over. I think I know where this spot is. I had to find him once, and he emerged from a thicket over by the creek. Am I right?" Jim said.

"Probably," Cory said. "I don't think I could find the place, but I can tell you if it's the right one."

When the boys got back with the jeep, all three dogs had jumped in.

"We won't all fit, guys," Jim scolded. Shadrach and Meshach obediently jumped out.

"We can fit with Abednego, can't we, Pops?" James pleaded.

The elderly man nodded with a smile, and they all loaded in. Jim drove them to the exact thicket that Z had taken her to.

"Is this it?" Jim asked.

"That's the one," She said.

Cory carefully picked her way into the clearing, motioning for the others to follow. They did.

"Wow! This is like a little fort!" James said with a touch of awe.

"It is," replied Cory as she retold the story Z had shared of finding the place. Just as it had when they were here, the ray of light was beaming through. Cory led the group to look at the red flower basking in the sunshine.

"It's just like my brother to find an amazing place like this. I always envied the relationship he had with God. I figured it was a reward for the difficult job he had been called to do," Abigail shared. "I'll have to remember to thank him for sharing it with us."

Gently, Cory checked under the leaves around the flower. There it was, the next clue.

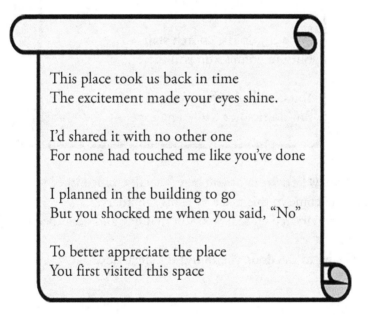

This place took us back in time
The excitement made your eyes shine.

I'd shared it with no other one
For none had touched me like you've done

I planned in the building to go
But you shocked me when you said, "No"

To better appreciate the place
You first visited this space

"He means the church, doesn't he?" put in Sarah.

"Well, kinda. But we went somewhere else first," she explained, then turned to Jim. "Just drive us to the church, and I'll show you."

When they got to the church, Cory led them around to the graveyard and told them all about the reason she wanted to go here. She pointed out the graves of interest and shared some of their conversation.

"I found it!" This time, it was Jim.

Lying beneath a small stone, up against a grave marker, Jim had found the next clue.

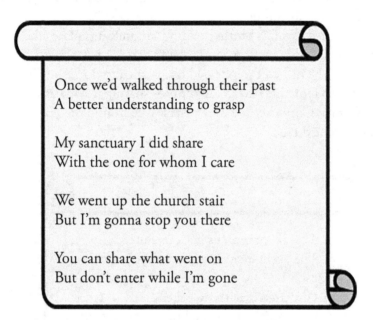

Once we'd walked through their past
A better understanding to grasp

My sanctuary I did share
With the one for whom I care

We went up the church stair
But I'm gonna stop you there

You can share what went on
But don't enter while I'm gone

"I knew he'd brought you here," Sarah chimed in. "He has never let anyone come in this place. It is his sanctuary."

Cory narrated all that went on that day and described the place to them all.

Going to the door, she found the next clue.

Something here went wrong
My feelings for you are so strong

My intentions you misunderstood
I thought I'd lost you for good

Yet you came in my time of need
You pointed me to Jesus and I was freed

Now I want you to know with no doubt
So go to the place and look out.

(Hint: I lift my eyes unto the hills from
        whence comes my help)

"What's that all about?" James asked.

Cory related the story of what Shelly had told her.

"I knew there was something wrong that day," Sarah said. "I just didn't know how to help you. I could tell you didn't want to share."

"I couldn't share. I was devastated," Cory explained.

"How could you believe someone like Shelly?" John questioned "With all that had happened between you and Uncle Z, how could you believe her over your own experiences?"

"John!" Abigail scolded.

"It's all right," Cory jumped in. "He's right. I just immediately believed her. I think—no, I know—I was already in disbelief of all that was happening. I just couldn't imagine how someone as amazing as Z could care for me. He is everything a girl could dream of and, well, I'm not. I was just ready to believe he could love Shelly because she is pretty."

Cory hung her head as Sarah placed an arm around her shoulders.

"I guess that's pretty shallow, but it's the truth," Cory admitted.

This time, it was Jim who spoke up. "Cory, you just have no idea how others see you. I think that is a part of what drew my son to you. You weren't trying to manipulate him. You were just being you. We all have our weak moments. Just learn from them."

Sarah hugged her tightly and said, "Where to next?"

"He took me to an overlook somewhere near here. We rode uphill for a while and came to a place with a cliff."

"I know where you are talking about. Get in," Jim offered.

Once again, the group piled in and headed to the spot. Sure enough, Jim knew where it was.

"I used to bring Granny here all the time. It's such a beautiful spot. We considered building our house up here but decided against it," Jim explained.

They all got out. It was indeed a beautiful view.

"Where's the next clue?" John queried.

Cory thought for a moment. "I lift my eyes unto the hills…" She walked over to the edge of the cliff and looked out at the hills in the distance.

"I wonder what he wanted me to see," she said, contemplating.

Her eyes scanned the horizon, then dropped to look over the edge of the cliff.

James and John followed her gaze. "What's down there?" they asked in unison.

They know something, Cory thought. She looked more pointedly below her. There, she noticed a flower. *He seemed to like flowers,* she thought. As she watched, another flower opened up.

Suddenly, a light bulb came on. "Hey, those are four o'clocks down there!" she exclaimed.

"What's a four o'clock?" John asked.

"My grandmother used to have them. They are flowers that open up every day at the same time," Cory answered.

"At four o'clock," James and John called out in unison.

As she watched, the flowers began to pop open. The seemingly random pattern began to take a shape.

"Look!" Cory exclaimed as realization swept over her. "That's the letter M."

The others moved to the edge and joined her. Each began calling out letters that they saw come in bloom. Soon, there at the foot of the cliff, spelled out in flowers was the last message.

WILL

YOU

MARRY

ME?

Cory stood there, stunned.

James and John whistled together. Abednego jumped up from his spot in the jeep. With some gesturing from the boys, he jumped over the side and ran to Cory.

He almost knocked her over but got her attention.

"What do you want?" she asked as she stooped to pet the dog. As she did, she felt an envelope around the dog's neck. Taking the envelope, she stood as she opened it.

The others standing around gathered in to see what she had in her hands.

It was empty.

She turned it over and…nothing.

Upon further examination, there was a hole in the bottom of the envelope. Whatever had been there must have fallen out.

A strange look came over Cory as she stood there holding the empty envelope. James and John stood wide eyed and in shock. No one moved for a moment.

Abednego broke the frozen silence. He began to bark uncontrollably and run in circles. Finally, he ran to the base of a tree and continued to leap and bark. The boys tried to quiet him, but he would have none of it.

"What's he barking at?" Abigail shouted above the din.

Just then, in a flurry of wings and feathers, a large bird flew from the tree.

"Look! It's an eagle! I told you they were back this year," James shouted.

As it flew majestically over, something fell from the bottom of it.

Cory was standing in shock. She was only vaguely aware of what was happening and had lifted her hands skyward palm up.

The object fell right into her hand.

She lowered her hand to look at it. There, in the palm of her hand, lay a beautiful diamond ring. She closed her fist around it and dropped to her knees as a tear trickled down her cheek.

Sarah was at her side in a moment.

"Are you okay?" she said, not sure what had just happened.

Cory merely raised her fist and opened her palm.

Sarah's hand flew to her mouth to cover her amazement. She dropped next to Cory and hugged her. Soon, the others had followed suit. Last but not least, Abednego jumped on the pile to officially make it a dog pile on Cory.

They all collapsed in laughter, joy, and tears.

When they finally gathered themselves, they loaded into the jeep and headed home.

Jim called Cory's father, and Abigail volunteered to go get him. When he arrived, they joined together to tell him all that had happened. After an enjoyable family dinner, they retired to the living room.

As the conversation began to wane, Cory lamented, "I only wish Z was here. I hope he comes home soon."

The others nodded in agreement and a hush fell over the group. Each one whispered a prayer for his safety.

It was Bob who broke the silence. Noticing the fatigue on Cory's face, he stood and said, "I think it's time we head home. It's been a big day, and Cory could use some rest."

With that, they rose and said their goodbyes, and Cory and Bob headed home.

Three weeks turned into six weeks, and six weeks became nine. Each day of silence held a mix of feelings: thankfulness because "no news is good news" and concern because every time the phone rang, it could be news he was dead and…hope…most of all hope that God was still in control. It was at times like this that she gloried in God's plan. She knew. Beyond the shadow of a doubt, she knew God was in control. As she thought back over her life, she only became more certain of it. That knowing made learning the lesson of trust more bearable. Because she knew God was in control, she could have the courage to trust. And trusting wasn't easy. That was a lesson she had to learn over and over again, but looking back, she could see the baby steps God had been walking her through. At the moment, she found comfort in rehearsing those steps one by one. It always left her amazed at God's goodness—reminding her what she knew—giving her courage to trust, and empowering her with hope to move on. Some people thought she was a fool for placing her faith in a book that was thousands of years old, but it was times like this when it became truly "a lamp unto her feet." She quoted to herself often,

> Be anxious for nothing but in everything through
> prayer with thanksgiving let your requests be made
> known unto God and the peace of God, which

passes all understanding will guard your hearts and
minds in Christ Jesus. (Philippians 4:6)

That's how she felt—guarded. The feelings swirled, but it wasn't
unsettling. She remembered God's goodness and was amazed. She
shared her fears with Him and was at peace. That doesn't mean she
wasn't affected. She was more like a duck on the pond, smoothly
floating on the surface but paddling hard underneath. She needed
God's peace, not once a day but hourly. Each time she'd begin to pad-
dle underneath, she would reach out to God, and He would wrap her
in peace. She didn't know how people handled this without God. She
figured that explained the broken families and hurting people she
often saw with the military. That, juxtaposed with the strong families
facing every tide together, were evidence to her of the fact that God
called some to the military and those He called He equipped.

Nine weeks stretched into six months. Still, she told no one in
her family. Oh, her father knew, but he shared nothing, respecting
her privacy. She was beginning to understand a little more clearly
what the Bible meant when it said, "she pondered all these things in
her heart." Granted, Mary had far more profound things to ponder,
but she found herself pondering.

Was God allowing this to test her? to strengthen her? Probably
yes to both of those.

Was God giving her those brief moments with Z to show her
what love was? that she could be loved? She hoped "no" to those if
they were final.

Was He preparing her to help others who struggled with fear
and grief? to help Z's family? No, hopefully, to those also.

Was He testing their faith to prepare them for the struggles
they would face together and yet apart? That was her request, but
she knew God's plan was really what she wanted. Though, often, it
hadn't matched her own, it had always been right, and it would be
right now.

School began after Labor Day, and Cory threw herself into her
class. When she began to catch herself worrying, she would whisper a
prayer and work grading papers, creating worksheets, and planning.

Absorbed in using her gifts, she was able to channel her worry into helping her students. They responded in just the way she needed—with love and cooperation and hard work. They noticed a change in her too. She was still fun but more focused. They were progressing through their curriculum at an impressive pace.

By November, still no word had come. Thanksgiving was coming, and it was time for the annual Thanksgiving meal. Every year, Cory had her class prepare an old-fashioned meal with all the fixin's. They stuffed the turkey, peeled the potatoes, snapped the beans, shucked the corn, and even churned homemade ice cream. It was quite a production and quite a learning experience—following directions, fractions, chemistry, and history galore! In all the excitement, you'd think she wouldn't have time for thoughts of Z, but she would look at her boys building picnic tables and benches for the dinner and picture him right there in the middle, winking at her as he helped "measure twice and cut once." The thought brought a smile to her face.

"A penny for your thoughts," broke in one of her students. She was a tall thin beautiful blonde senior, and she had known Cory since birth. Their families weren't joined by blood; they were bound by something just as deep—maybe deeper. They had met at church and served God together for years. They were family by Spirit and choice. Danyelle could read Cory like a book, but she didn't know about Z.

Cory thought for a minute, then answered, "I was just imagining something that made me smile." Honesty was best. Danyelle would know if she made something up.

"Well, with a smile like that, I want to know what you were imagining." She giggled with excitement.

"Okay, picture this. Standing over there, helping the boys, a man not much over six feet tall, with dark skin and curly dark hair. He's muscularly built and not a stranger to hard work. He looks up, and as a big toothy smile spreads across his face, you peer into probably the most beautiful blue eyes you've ever seen, and just when you think you'll drown in those eyes, he winks at you and goes back to work." Cory knew Danyelle would never believe she was describing a very possible scenario, so she felt no fear in telling her.

Danyelle excitedly took Cory by the elbow, and with girlish enthusiasm said, "I'll take one of those too, please." She waited a bit, then lowered her voice to just above a whisper so only Cory could hear, and with a maturity and concern far beyond her years said, "I don't know what's been going on with you lately, but I want you to know that God is at work and because I love you, I've been praying for you."

With that, she squeezed Cory's arm, gave her a quick kiss on the cheek, and headed back to the kitchen.

Cory turned to watch her go just as Danyelle's younger sister Len shouted from the kitchen, "Danyelle, it's your turn to crank the ice cream. I'm getting tired!"

Danyelle picked up the pace and disappeared into the kitchen.

God had indeed been good to Cory. Though she never had children of her own, she had been able to be with these two girls and their family through all the stages of growing up. What an honor it had been to be allowed by their parents to be so close. She had gotten a taste, if only a small, outsider's one, of what it was like to have kids. She remembered the awe of holding Danyelle when she was only hours old after being born at home. She thought fondly of the girls learning to walk and talk and calling her name. She even ruefully recollected the fear when they got away from her or went off on their own. Because of this precious family, Cory had never felt alone. God had seen to that.

She found herself pleading with God for those girls to get to meet Z. She wanted so badly for them to choose to follow God all their lives, to trust Him when making choices about relationships. If they could see the amazing way God had brought Cory and Z together, there's no way they would walk away from God.

That's not true, Cory silently scolded herself. *God, I'm sorry for wanting to orchestrate their lives. I know that true love for You can't be created because of manipulation. It comes ultimately from You, but if You could—if it's in Your plan—I promise to let everyone I know that only a God so loving, glorious, and strong could help an old spinster like me find true love!* She smiled as she almost felt God say "I know, that's why I chose you."

With that, she hurried into the kitchen herself to check on the meal's progress.

The kitchen was alive with activity. Normally, this meal happened during school hours and was a free lunch. The school was growing, so this year—at the last minute—the parents had talked her into a fundraiser dinner. This school was the culmination of a dream, and God continued to amaze them all. It was modeled after schools in the pioneer days of America when all the parents in a town would band together and hire a teacher who would run a one-room school house. It offered a place for parents who were frustrated with the public school system but couldn't afford private school or weren't able to home school. The students read original historical documents and learned by doing and discussed the things of God. They even used some old textbooks written by Daniel Webster. It was truly a student-centered teacher-driven model, and the waiting list grew every year. The price was low because the school only had to support one class and one teacher. To do that, the class was the teacher's home.

For events like tonight, Cory's church allowed the use of their facilities. So here they were, bustling around a huge kitchen, decorating a huge hall, and building picnic tables outside—all while learning.

For some, the juggling act and noise would be frustrating, but to Cory, it was amazing to see these kids work together—the older ones teaching the younger ones—and as a team, accomplishing a tremendous feat they and their parents could enjoy.

In what seemed like a matter of minutes but was really a couple of hours, the room was buzzing with tables full of happy people enjoying a delicious meal. It seemed lit by the faces of her students, glowing with pride as they waited tables and received praise for their hard work. Once everything seemed stable, Cory and her students fixed themselves plates and took their seats to join the fellowship. As she surveyed the room, it seemed everyone she knew was here—friends from this school, from church, and even some from churches where she had served before. Boy, they had gotten the word out!

Over in the corner, she spotted her father at a table with the Christians—Jim and Sarah, Abigail and the boys were all here. *Daddy must have invited them*, she thought. The two men had become good friends, so that made her smile.

Just as she was about to get up and go over to their table, her sister stood.

"May I have everyone's attention please," she began. "I want to thank all of you for coming tonight. We know how important this school is, so thank you for your generosity. We also know that none of this would be possible without some really hard work by a person we all love. Cory, will you come up here please."

The group applauded, and some of her students cheered "That's my teacher" as she stood and moved forward. When she reached the front, her sister gave her a hug and then held onto her arm.

When the applause died down, she continued, "What Cory doesn't know, and what some of the rest of you might not know, is that we have an ulterior motive. Something wonderful has happened recently in Cory's life, and we want to share it with you."

Cory froze. She wasn't ready. *What if Z was killed in action and never came back?*

She wasn't ready to handle all the sympathy.

She tried to catch her sister's eye and send a "*stop!*" look, but she seemed to be avoiding her gaze.

"We all know that God has had a hold of Cory's life. Some of us have watched it and been involved for a long time. He's done it again. He has done what many of us have prayed for." She turned to Cory, now looking her directly in the eye and ignoring all the nonverbal cues Cory was flooding her with.

"Cory, I know that I once accused you of being the pope and unable to understand what others felt when they fell in love. I know you're not, but"—she looked back at the audience—"you know how sisters can be when they're fighting."

The crowd laughed.

"I really didn't understand how you could be so calm alone. I just had to accept that it was just who you had chosen to be. I watched you trust God, and I wanted that too. But in the back of my mind, I wanted you to experience what I found in my marriage and family. And just like He always does with you, He snuck up on us all." She turned back to the audience. "God sent Cory a godly man!"

The room erupted in applause. There were even some squeals from her girls. Cory was speechless. She looked to the Christians' table. Sarah was beaming. James and John stood and approached.

"Before she can say anything, and because I know some of you are in shock right now, I have video proof. These two young men, James and John, videoed the important moment, and I'm glad they did because if they hadn't, I wouldn't believe the story. It's too incredible, but it's exactly what I expect from God for my sis. Take it away, boys."

As the boys set up a projector to shoot on the wall, Cory felt a hand on her shoulder. Danyelle had come up behind her with a chair for her to sit in. Setting it down, she embraced Cory and whispered in her ear, "That explains a lot." She let go and looked her in the eye. "Were you describing him earlier?"

Cory nodded. "Think of an older version of those two." She whispered, indicating the twins. Danyelle looked over, then back. The twinkle in her eye matched the one in Cory's.

"God is good!" she said.

Cory replied, "All the time!"

Danyelle sat at Cory's feet as the projector began. There, before her eyes and the eyes of her friends and family, unfolded the unbelievable account of the proposal. As she watched what unfolded, she found herself unconsciously reaching for and holding the ring, which hung on a chain around her neck. Watching it was like watching one of those sappy Christmas movies on Hallmark. As she watched, she reexperienced all the emotions. She heard the "Ahs" in the crowd and even a "No way!" or two. When it was done, the room erupted.

When they quieted down, she felt the need to reign in their excitement. One of her students provided the opportunity. "How come you didn't tell us?" Len asked

"Where's the ring?" Danyelle asked. "I want to see that ring."

The crowd fell silent, waiting for her to answer.

"Well," she began, "wow, watching that was almost more unbelievable than living it!"

She looked down at Danyelle who pointed to her ring finger and tapped on it.

"Let me see if I can explain. I'm not wearing the ring because… well, I remember vividly after reading the message in flowers asking God if this was His plan. I was filled with the desire for Z—that's what I call him—to have the woman God had for him. I wanted that to be me, but it seemed too incredible. All I could think was how he deserved more than me. I remember praying for God to help me know how I should answer and to give me a definite, clear sign what my answer should be.

"When I opened that envelope, and it was empty, my heart fell. I think it was obvious that I was in shock. I really felt that this was God's way of telling me I wasn't supposed to get married. At that moment, I believed God was telling me to say no to the proposal."

Cory looked at her sister and then to the table where her father and the Christians sat. The look on their faces was the same. Stunned. Abigail leaned over to her mother and whispered, "She never did accept the proposal out loud. You don't think…"

Reading her lips, Cory hurried to finish.

"At that moment, I began to pray. I surrendered to whatever God's plan was. I don't know if you can back it up, but if you can, you will see on the video, I was standing with my hands lifted, palms up. I had completely surrendered and—I swear this is true—said, 'God, unless you do something spectacular at this moment to show me what only You could do, I'm going to decline this proposal.' No sooner had I said that in my spirit than that eagle flew over and dropped that ring in the palm of my hand. I just stood there. Only God could have done that! Oh, Z and the boys orchestrated an amazing proposal, but God gave me the ring."

The group broke into applause. When it died down, she continued.

"I didn't say anything about it to most of you because I can't introduce him to you. You'll notice he wasn't in the video either. That's because he's not here. He's in the military and on active duty.

For almost the last year, he's been overseas. He's in the Special Forces, so I don't know when or if he'll return. I wanted him to be with me—maybe so you'd believe me." She chuckled.

At that moment, a commotion began in the back of the room. The sounds of a guitar playing filled the room. There, holding a guitar, stood Z. He was still in his fatigues, and as he moved through the room toward her, he sang,

> *All of my life, I have dreamed somehow love would*
> *find me.*
> *Now I can't believe you're standing here.*
> *If beauty is all in the eye of the beholder*
> *Then I wish you could see the love for you that lives*
> *in me.*

As his strong baritone filled the space between them, tears filled Cory's eyes. When he reached the chorus, she crossed the space between them with her voice and sang with him. These two voices, separated by the space of a large room, united in unison as the rest of the people in the room became silent spectators, watching God bring two of His children together.

> *Then you would know you have my heart.*
> *If you could see what I see.*
> *That a treasure is what you are*
> *If you could see what I see*
> *Created to be the only one for me*
> *If you could see what I see.*

Approaching her, their eyes met. There in the bright blue of his eyes and the deep blue of hers, the pure love that only God can bestow poured through their hearts and to one another. In that moment, all doubt, fear, and inhibition vanished as he continued to sing. The words pierced directly to her soul as both God and this incredible man tapped into those deep insecurities that every woman fights.

I know there are days when you feel so much less
than ideal
Wondering what I see in you.
It's all of the light and the grace, your belief in me
drives me to say,
That I promise you a faithful love forever true.

Again, Cory joined, this time, in harmony. The two distinctly unique children of God brought their differences together. The dark timber of his deep voice carried the melody as the bright high tones of hers added a beautiful enhancement to the words. They sang with a passion fueled by the love they knew from the Lord and offered to one another.

When he began singing the bridge, he dropped to his knee, and she choked back tears of pure delight.

Then you'd understand why I fall down to my knees
And I pray my love will be worthy of the One who
gave his life
So our love could be
If you could see what I see.
If you could see what I see.
You're created to be the perfect one for me.
If you could see what I see.

Z set his guitar aside and reached his hand up for her. Cory took that hand and knelt with him. Tears were streaming down her face, and he wiped them from her cheek with his other hand. Peering deeply in each other's eyes, they finished the song, acapella, in harmony.

If beauty is all in the eye of the beholder, then I am
beholding true beauty.

As they embraced one another, the room erupted in applause. Some of her students cheered, and her sister let out her signature whistle.

As the two embraced on the stage, Z whispered in her ear, "You know the song!"

Sniffling back emotion, she whispered back. "I heard that song when Geoff Moore sang it after Steven Curtis Chapman helped him write it. I went out and bought it because I told God that when I found a man who could sing this to me, I would know He was behind it."

A smile spread across Z's face, and the watery evidence of tears lined the bottom of his baby blues. "You're kidding. I heard it and told God that if I could ever feel this way about a woman and have the courage to sing it to her, I would know He had brought her to me."

The two embraced. With a quick move, Z pulled back, and a worried look flitted across his face.

"Hey, wait a minute. Where's the ring? Standing back there, I was beginning to think you would say no. Why aren't you wearing it?"

It would seem Cory's smile couldn't get any bigger, but it did. She reached for a chain around her neck. "It's right here. I decided to wear it close to my heart until you could put it on my finger."

Relief, then joy washed over him. With nimble fingers, he unclasped the necklace and slid the ring from it.

"Then let me take care of that right now. Cory Carter, will you marry me?"

Cory extended her hand, and Z placed the ring on her finger.

"Yes, of course, yes!" she said through tears.

One of Cory's students shouted from across the room, "Kiss her!"

Z stood and, with his hand, guided her to her feet. "That sounds like a good idea to me. What do you think?"

Cory didn't wait to answer. She wrapped her arms around his neck, and with absolutely no inhibition, she stretched up on her tiptoes and gently placed her lips on his. He knew instantly what that meant and responded. He slipped his arms around her waist and raised her from the floor. Love washed away any fear or discomfort as they surrendered to one another and God's will for their lives.

The room again erupted as those who cared so deeply about these two watched what every one of them knew was a perfect picture of God's desire for the love of a man and a woman. Before them, they saw a couple who had individually surrendered their lives to Christ and chosen to follow Him. They had come to know His love and trust His heart. Now, He had brought them together to discover together the beautiful gift God has given mankind in the love between a man and a woman. They dared to believe God with their lives and now stood as proof that regardless of what the world put forth, God's plan was better.

If they had been able to see into the heavenlies, they would have seen a smile cross the face of God Himself. And if they looked closely into the eyes of the King of the Universe, they would see what only He could see. There, deeply in the fertile soil of the heart of each and every one of them—and especially in the hearts of the teenagers and children—a seed was planted. Oh, that seed would be battered by the voices that would scream it didn't exist. It would be nearly starved as the atmosphere around it filled with millions of images claiming to know the truth of what love is.

But it had taken root.

Through the years, they—if they would listen—would hear His whisper.

No matter the *world's* attempts, they could—if they would—come to know the love He had for them and find the one He had prepared.

If they would.

Their stories now wait to be told, and only God knows how they will be written.

ABOUT THE AUTHOR

Constance Cooper has been a youth minister and school teacher for over thirty years. In that time, she continuously encountered two recurring problems among the teenagers she worked with: an insatiable hunger to be loved and a repulsion to reading. After one student admitted that she had never read an entire book, Constance made a deal that would change everything. If she wrote a book, the student agreed to read it cover to cover. Here, she found her chance to address the two problems she had identified. Through writing, she could help people see that God's *love* is the one that will satisfy their hunger, and by developing a love for reading, they can begin to move from novels to the One Book that will help them discover the truth and depth of that love—the Bible. From her home in a small town in Texas, she continues to teach at Cooper Christian Academy, lead music at Williams Road Baptist Church, and encourage everyone she meets to discover two great loves of their own: reading and Almighty God!